JACK AND THE GENIUSES

IN THE DEEP BLUE SEA

BILL NYE
& GREGORY MONE

ILLUSTRATED BY
NICK ILUZADA

AMULET BOOKS • NEW YORK

JACK AND THE GENIUSES

IN THE DEEP BLUE SEA

CATALOGING-IN-PUBLICATION DATA HAS BEEN APPLIED FOR
AND MAY BE OBTAINED FROM THE LIBRARY OF CONGRESS.
ISBN 978-1-4197-2552-4

ABRAMS The Art of Books
195 Broadway, New York, NY 10007
abramsbooks.com

FOR OCEAN EXPLORERS EVERYWHERE,
LEARN THE SECRETS OF THE SEA
AND SEEK ADVENTURE!

—B.N.

TO ELEANOR

—G.M.

CONTENTS

1. INSIDE THE UNDERPLANE 1

2. THE BAZILLIONAIRE'S BABY 16

3. WE'RE NOT ENTERTAINMENT 37

4. HE WHO BATHES BENEATH
   WATERFALLS 54

5. HAWKING HEADQUARTERS 69

6. A DANGEROUS DECISION 89

7. TWO THOUSAND FEET DOWN 100

8. AN AQUATIC INVESTIGATION 114

9. MRS. WINTERBOTTOM'S MOLARS 128

10. THE GLIMMER AND THE GULL 140

11. A PARTY FOR A PRINCE 153

12. THE BRUTAL BREATH OF
    PAKA'A 176

13. SPIDER SAILING 191

14. ANSWERS IN THE STARS 202

15. FRANK TO THE RESCUE 216

16. THE REAL SABOTEUR 231

17. CRIMINALLY SHAPED 241

18. THE ART OF WAR 252

19. OPERATION TURKISH DELIGHT 274

20. AN ABSOLUTE WRECK 291

ELEVEN ABSOLUTELY ESSENTIAL
QUESTIONS ABOUT THE DEEP
BLUE SEA 298

OUR BIG BLUE OCEAN—
AN EXPERIMENT BY BILL NYE 304

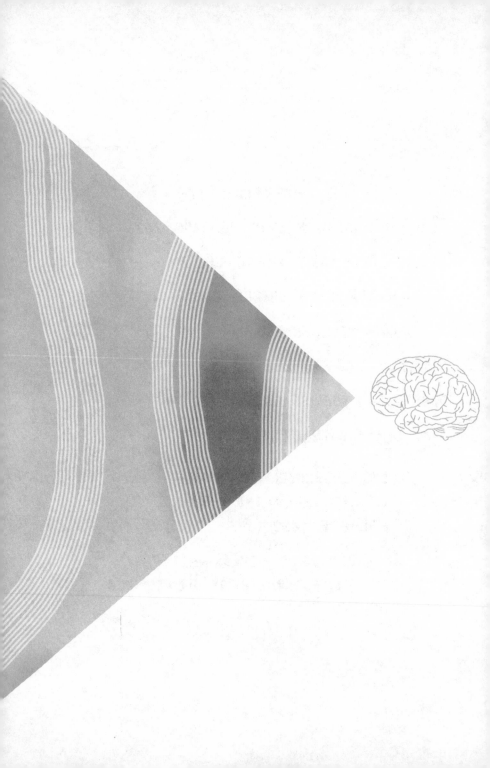

I

INSIDE THE UNDERPLANE

THE CLIFFS OF NIHOA ISLAND STOOD TALL AS WE soared above the calm blue water. *Nihoa* means "toothed" in Hawaiian, but the jagged mass of gray-green rock jutting up out of the Pacific Ocean looked like the rotten molar of a sea monster. We were flying low in a small six-seater airplane, and I really, really didn't want to crash into that tooth. For about the fifteenth time, I checked my seat belt.

Our pilot, the bazillionaire computer scientist Ashley Hawking, was rambling about the annoying birds that nested on the island. But I didn't care about finches or swallows. An eagle could have chest-bumped my window and it would not have shifted my focus. If we continued on our current course, we were going to smash into the jagged wall like an egg launched from a slingshot.

The plane's engine roared.

My stomach spun.

1

Next to me, my brother was staring straight ahead, eyes bulging, with his thin black notebook computer open on his lap. I grabbed his shoulder. His muscles were as solid as rocks and his face was a greenish shade of white. "Matt?" I asked. "Is she pulling up?"

His mouth barely opened. "I hope so," he mumbled.

Our sister, Ava, was sitting in the row behind us, watching the flashing red and green numbers on the electronic control panel. A vein on the side of her head pulsed. She didn't notice me staring back at her. Meanwhile, Ashley Hawking was grinning so wide I could see the edges of her smile from my seat directly behind her. Our mentor, the geek-famous inventor Henry Witherspoon, or Hank, glanced back at me from the co-pilot's seat, his awkward smile flashing too many teeth. Was he trying to make us feel better? If so, he was failing.

Hank leaned over to Ashley. He held his hand out flat and swooped it up toward the roof of the cockpit. "Should we, you know, ascend?"

"What?" Hawking asked. "No! Of course not. Ascend? I thought you knew!"

"Knew what?"

Hawking let go of the controls and waved her hands in a sweeping motion. She sighed with disappointment. "This is one of yours!"

"One of my what?" Hank asked.

"One of your designs!"

Hank spun in his seat, scanning the interior. His mouth was all bunched to one side. He was squinting. And he was completely stumped. Only Hank Witherspoon would struggle to recognize one of his own inventions. His mind was so productive that he dropped out new ideas with about as much thought as a chicken laying eggs.

Matt reached forward with one of his long arms and pointed. "Ummm . . . cliff?"

"What was that?" Hawking yelled back.

We couldn't have been more than a few football fields away from the rock wall. "I think he's wondering if we're planning to avoid that cliff," I said.

Below us, out the left side of the plane and far from the island, a large dock with two boats tied to the sides floated in the middle of the ocean. The water was neon blue and smooth as glass. We probably could've landed on it, but I hadn't noticed any pontoons when we climbed into the aircraft that morning. The thing clearly wasn't a seaplane. So the only safe choices were up, right, or left. And if Ashley Hawking didn't pick one of those soon, we'd keep heading straight. Into the cliffs. We'd be smashed to bits, and all the headlines would read, "Four Geniuses Die as Plane Crashes into Tooth."

3

No, I wouldn't be the fourth. That honor would belong to Ashley Hawking. The world would mourn the loss of the two accomplished adults and my brilliant brother and ingenious sister. Me? I might be mentioned in the story somewhere, but I'm no brainiac. I'm average. Maybe a little above, but not by much, and only through effort. I have to work hard, and read all the time, to keep up with the geniuses.

But anyway. Back to that nasty nine-hundred-foot-tall cliff sticking straight up out of the water in front of us. Maybe the *Millennium Falcon* could have made the turn, swooping up at the last second, but I wasn't liking our chances. "Ms. Hawking?"

"Ashley! I told you already. Ashley. And not because I think of you as an equal. Not at all." She laughed to herself. "I simply prefer the sound of my first name. Now, honestly, Hank, someone of your intelligence . . . I assumed you'd see."

Hank was panicking now, his head turning from side to side in jerks, like a broken sprinkler. "I don't . . . when . . ."

Suddenly my sister leaned forward and pointed at a large orange button in the ceiling, covered by a clear plastic case. "Are you serious?" she said with excitement. "Is this the underplane?"

"Yes!" Ashley fake head-butted the dashboard a few times, then looked up to the ceiling. "The child gets the answer. Finally!"

Although Ava was relieved, I found this news to be more than a little frightening. "You made a plane out of underwear?" I asked.

The moment the words escaped I realized I'd probably misunderstood. But no one noticed. Or at least no one bothered to make fun of me. Not yet, anyway. Ava and Matt were pretty skilled at remembering my mistakes, though.

"This is the underplane?" Hank asked. His eyebrows rose so high they nearly touched the top of his head. "You actually built it?"

"I did. But enough talk. You're right, Jack," she said, swiveling around to look me in the eye. "We are getting awfully close, aren't we?" I nodded. The acknowledgment was nice, but I really wanted her to turn back around. "Are we buckled? Good. Would you like to do the honors, Hank?"

"You've tested it?"

"Of course! Once. But it worked beautifully. Go ahead. Press it. Do it. Now."

"You've only tested it once?"

5

On the dashboard between them, a number in the center of the screen was blinking red and decreasing rapidly. "Yes, once, and a thousand times in simulation. Be confident in your ideas, Hank! Press the button already." She pointed to the flashing red number, which just kept dropping. "Really. Now. Three hundred meters is pushing things. I haven't felt this much adrenaline since I climbed Everest."

Matt mumbled something about the cliff.

Hank hesitated.

Ashley had Manga eyes.

I don't know what Ava was thinking or doing.

But this was no time to sit and wait. I slouched forward in my seat, reached up with my right foot, flicked open the plastic covering, and kicked in the orange button with the heel of my high-top sneaker.

Ashley let out a long, almost disappointed breath. "Finally," she said.

Hank had his right hand out, three fingers extended. He counted down from three. A moment later, the engine stalled. The aircraft turned strangely quiet, as if we were suddenly flying in a giant paper plane.

"Now the chute?" Ava asked.

Before anyone could respond, something exploded behind us.

Yet nobody but me panicked.

Ava put her hand on my shoulder. "A rocket-launched parachute," she explained. "Don't worry. That was supposed to happen."

Firing a parachute out with a rocket didn't make sense to me, but the plane slowed, rattling like an old roller coaster, then began circling to the left. Away from the cliffs. So I exhaled. The lonely floating dock came into view ahead of us. Out through the window, I noticed two wooden boats rounding the corner of the island. Matt was staring at his computer screen again, mumbling to himself. He had a big test coming up, and he'd been studying constantly. One of the downsides of being a genius is that everyone expected you to ace all your tests. I don't think Hank cared, though. Matt put more pressure on himself than anyone else did. But was this really a good time to prepare for an astronomy exam? No. So I reached across and closed his laptop. He didn't protest, which was pretty much a thank-you.

"Wow, it works," Ava said.

"I told you I'd tested it."

"Yeah, once," Ava noted.

"And a thousand times in simulation," Hank added.

The others laughed. Apparently this was funny.

Normally I avoided asking for an explanation when everyone else understood. Hank was always saying there's no such thing as a dumb question, but I was pretty sure I

7

proved him wrong twice a day. And I hated reminding them that I lived on a lower level of the brain game. But there were times I needed to know. "What does 'in simulation' mean?"

Ashley looked back at me like I'd just asked the difference between salt and pepper.

"It's a computerized version of reality, Jack," Hank explained.

"It's like the difference between Street Racer and an actual street race, with real cars," Ava added.

Now I understood. She knew how to speak my language. See, I was actually kind of awesome at Street Racer, and I had this feeling that I'd be a sick driver in the real world, too.

A brown, wide-winged bird swooped in front of us. "Is that a petrel?" Matt asked.

"They're frequent visitors to the island," Ashley said.

Great. Now they were bird-watching, and yet we were still in a plane without pontoons, gliding over the ocean without any clear runway in sight. Sure, we were finally descending, but the underplane turned about as easily as the *Titanic*. As we swung closer to the cliff, I held my breath. No one spoke. I'm not sure anyone even breathed. Ashley and Hank leaned to their left, as if that might help, and the tip of our right wing passed within ten feet of the rocks. Next to me, Matt's face was still that greenish-white color, and

8

he was breathing carefully and gripping the armrests with enough force to dent them.

"That was close!" Ashley said, her voice more excited than relieved.

"So, umm, what's next?" I asked.

"Well, you see, this is the first phase of the transition," Hank said. "The first parachute allows for a more gradual descent, but there's also a braking chute to slow us down further."

"And then?" I pressed.

Hank's eyebrows arched twice. "Wait and see," he said.

Ava tapped me on the shoulder. "Don't worry, I think you're going to like this. It is called 'the underplane,' after all."

I still didn't get what boxers or briefs had to do with the five of us landing safely. But I wasn't about to ask. "So, about that braking chute . . . can we use it now?"

"Not until we slow to thirty miles per hour."

Hank cocked his head to the side, struggling for a view of the parachute suspended above us. "Amazing. Truly. I don't know how to thank you, Ashley. I never thought anyone would ever build one."

The plane soared through a wide loop. We were still about the height of a four-story building from the glassy sea. We swung toward the rock face of Nihoa again, only this time at half the speed and with much less chance of crashing. The color in Matt's face had not changed, but I knew better than to ask him how he was feeling. When Matt was hurt or sick, he didn't want anyone to know. He'd rather hide off by himself somewhere than let you see him aching.

The two boats came into view again. They looked like museum pieces. The masts were tall, the sails all rolled up, and a few people on either side were digging into the water with long black paddles. "What are those?" I asked.

Ashley Hawking squinted, gagged for a three-count, then breathed in, shook her head, and smiled. "Friends of mine," she said. "They think we're enemies, but as I'm sure you know, kids, those two are one and the same. As Sun Tzu said, you should treat your enemies as if they are your best friends."

"Is he one of those jazz guys, Hank?" I asked. Our mentor had strange taste in music, but I was growing to like some of the tunes. I'd been trying to learn their names to impress him.

"No, that's Sun Ra, and he only really began as a jazz pianist—"

Another jolt cut his answer short. Ava pointed to the control panel. Our speed was dropping rapidly. And we were circling closer and closer to the water. Hank turned. I thought he was checking to see if we were okay, but he stared out the small rearview window instead. His smile vanished. "You used a larger braking chute."

"Yes," Ashley said. "I had to. In simulation, the chute you suggested didn't slow the plane quickly enough. Your design was completely inadequate. No offense."

Hank paused before answering. "None taken?"

We were at least a few city blocks away from the island, gliding through our third full circle, cruising at the speed of a bike down a steep hill, when the plane finally skimmed the surface of the sea.

We bounced.

Hank whooped.

Ashley hollered.

Then we bounced again and again, lower each time, like a stone skipping across the water.

Ava quietly beamed, and my still-green brother relaxed his grip. When we finally stopped, my heart was thumping. My hands were cramped. Apparently, Matt wasn't the only one squeezing the armrests. I looked out the window. We had to be a mile away from the shore. Was this really the right place to land? Were we floating? Or sinking? And what did all this have to do with underwear?

Ecstatic, Hank pointed to the button on the roof, then asked Ashley, "May I?"

"You're the guest," Ashley said.

11

Hank pushed the button with the heel of his hand. Above me, something clicked. A thud followed, somewhere behind us. Then two loud hisses on either side of the plane. Below me, I heard the sound of rushing water, like a quickly filling toilet bowl. Suddenly I needed to go to the bathroom, but there were more important things happening.

Glancing out the window, I noticed that the wings were dropping below the surface. The plane was sinking. And no one else onboard seemed particularly bothered. "This is supposed to happen?" I asked.

Matt pointed his thumb out the window and swallowed. "Why not shed the wings?" he asked, struggling to get the words out.

"The aerodynamic profile of the wings is hydrodynamically efficient, too," Hank answered. "In both cases, you're just moving through a fluid."

Ava put her hand on my shoulder. She wore several colorful beaded rings. "What he means," she began, leaning forward, "is that you don't need to drop the wings because—"

"I know," I said. And I didn't, really, but the geniuses are always explaining things to me, and I wasn't in the mood for a lesson. So I pulled out my new notebook. Before we'd left for Hawaii I had a great idea. Or a great idea for me, anyway. Whenever the geniuses said something I didn't understand, I'd jot down a little note about it, then do some research later and learn about it on my own. That way I wouldn't have to admit it when I wasn't following along. And sure, I could've checked on my phone, but then they'd notice. I held the notebook down in the space between my left leg and the side of the plane, so Matt couldn't see, and scribbled "hydrodynamic" on a blank page. After a second, I added "Sun Something"—unfortunately, I'd already forgotten the name of the guy Ashley quoted.

The plane was sinking faster. The dock with the two boats was only a few pool lengths away; part of me wished we could've just swum over. But the blue water was already climbing up the sides. The surface reached the bottom of my window, then rose higher and higher until it climbed over the top. A few seconds later, the underplane dropped below the surface and began gliding down through the blue sea.

Oh.

Right.

The *underplane*. As in *underwater plane*. Not an aircraft made out of old boxer shorts.

Our ride had transformed into a six-seat submarine.

Since we met Hank seven months ago, I'd been introduced to all kinds of strange machines and vehicles and experiences. I'd been to the bottom of the world and fought off a crazy Australian and flown in an inflatable vehicle that wasn't supposed to fly. I'd even had some experiences with

13

miniature subs, since my sister had built one. But I'd never been inside an actual submarine. And certainly not in the Pacific Ocean, with who knows how much water or how many deadly creatures lurking below me. On the one-to-ten scale of soul-stretching, brain-twisting experiences, I'd give this one a fourteen.

The water was filled with specks that sparkled in the sunlight. A group of long silver fish darted past our windows. I'd always imagined that riding in a submarine would be like staring at the fish tanks in an aquarium. But now it felt as if we were the ones trapped in the tank. And I kind of wanted to get back to the air. "So that was fun," I said, "but can we go back up now?"

My ears popped.

"Up? Of course not," Ashley said.

The underplane nosed down in the direction of the island. But we weren't going to Nihoa. Not yet. Far below us, an enormous, brightly lit underwater building hung below the dock. It looked like the headquarters of some kind of powerful secret society or nefarious villain. The outside was swarming with huge fish.

"You still want to go back up, Jack?" Ava asked.

I could practically hear her smiling. "No," I said with a grin. "Not anymore."

2

THE BAZILLIONAIRE'S BABY

YOU PROBABLY KNOW ME. OR THE OTHERS, ANYWAY. If you haven't read *The Lonely Orphans*, the best-selling book of poems my brother and sister wrote about us, then you might have seen the news about our recent adventure in Antarctica. That whole thing was supposed to be a secret. But when three kids and their brilliant mentor rescue a missing scientist and her world-changing discovery from a frozen wasteland, the public has a right to know. And if one of those kids accidentally sent all the details of that adventure to a few major reporters and minor Twitter gods, the others shouldn't have gotten so mad. They shouldn't have accused this innocent young individual of spreading the story because they believed his—or her—only goal was to win fame and fortune.

That would be unfair.

Mean, really.

And besides, what's wrong with fame and fortune?

I certainly won't tell you which one of us was the guilty party in that whole fiasco. Instead, we'll move on with our lives and this story, which started a few days before our ride in the underplane. Ava, Matt, and I are foster siblings. Although we're kids—Ava and I are twelve, and Matt recently turned sixteen—we're actually adults in the eyes of the law. I know. It's weird. And it definitely confuses people, so I'll run through the basics. A little more than a year ago, we divorced our foster parents and convinced a judge to let us live on our own. Now we share a small apartment in Brooklyn, and a Social Services appointed lady named Min checks on us every so often to make sure we're alive and functioning. Ava and I homeschool through online programs, with a little added help from Hank. Matt just started his first year of college. Biologically, we're not related, and we definitely don't look anything like siblings. Matt towers over the both of us. His hair is short and dark and he always has a slight tan. His large nose looks like it was carved by a chisel, and although he has the build of an athlete, the guy can't cross a room without bumping into something. Ava has coffee-colored skin; wide, bright eyes; and hair that's always yanked back in a ponytail. She insists she's taller than me, but I'm catching up. I'm easily the best-dressed member of our group, and I doubt either of them would disagree that I've got the best hair, too.

17

Most of the time, we hang out at Hank's private lab. It's only a few blocks from our place, and it's pretty much the world's coolest clubhouse. A towering, wide-open space ten stories tall, Hank's lab is filled with technological toys. He has self-driving cars, motorized chairs, and a catapult designed to launch people instead of boulders. (Which doesn't actually work.) There are robots that crawl, walk, jump, fly, and even serve you pizza. One of the rooms is a perfect replica of the surface of Mars, only with normal gravity. And there's a massive dive tank for testing submarines and SCUBA suits. You're definitely not supposed to swim around in the tank, though—not even when he's away on a trip.

Also, this confuses people, but Hank's not our dad. He's not just a teacher or a mentor or guide, though, either. I don't know how to explain it, exactly. He's just . . . Hank. And although he does a lot for us, we don't just run around the lab for fun. We help him out, too, and as a kind of reward, he took us down to the bottom of the world with him a little while back. What was supposed to be a kind of science-themed vacation turned into a pretty dangerous adventure. But that's another story.

After we returned from that South Pole trip, we were just lying around the apartment in Brooklyn, recuperating, when Hank surprised us by inviting us on this journey. We asked a million questions. Why were we going? What for?

Would we ride on a private jet? Okay, so that was my question. We'd taken one part of the way to the South Pole, and it was truly glorious.

Hank didn't have too many answers for us, but only one thing really mattered to me: We'd been invited to Hawaii. Palm trees, pineapples, ridiculous shirts? I was ready to go right then and there. My siblings, though, were a little more curious. Matt and Ava pressed Hank with questions about who needed our help and why. Hank told us what he knew, but he filled it with way too many science and engineering terms.

Here's my version: A very wealthy computer geek named Ashley Hawking had given a bunch of money to a young engineer who had some crazy new plan for generating electricity. Hawking tossed thirty million dollars at the project, and once it was working beautifully, she organized this big public demonstration, with Hawaiian politicians and leading businesspeople and ribbons and these cool flowered leis and maybe even people in grass skirts—I don't know, I'm just guessing about that part. Anyway, the electricity plant totally flunked. So Ashley was totally embarrassed, and she and the engineer looked into what went wrong, and not long after that they invited us out.

Got it? Okay. Good.

As for why we got the invite, Hank suspected it was

his own reputation as a problem solver, but I have a different theory. I think Ashley and her engineer friend were the victims of sabotage. And they probably read those news stories based on that innocent kid's leaks and figured we could solve their mystery, too. Either way, whether it was a simple engineering flaw or a devious plot, we'd be able to help. Hank is a world-class scientist and inventor, and my siblings are getting smarter by the minute. They ask all the right questions and chase the answers like a pair of border collies racing after a tossed Frisbee. As for yours truly, I'd been teaching myself more about the detective trade. Through a few thick books, mostly. But I'd also learned a surprising amount from a new animated series, *Duck Detective*, about a very resourceful fowl who solves mysteries on a crowded country farm.

Anyway, the cool part is that Ashley specifically requested that we join Hank. She truly wanted our help, which made Matt and Ava about as happy as two goats at a salad bar. And I was curious, too. While the rest of them studied this electricity plant, I was going to find the crook who was trying to sabotage the project.

We flew out to California first. On a regular old commercial plane, unfortunately. I sat next to a woman whose nostrils fluttered when she snored. Her breath smelled like a burrito, and I used the time to skim two books about Hawaii and a short novel about an old fisherman that Hank

insisted I read. I also watched a few very instructive episodes of *Duck Detective*. Two hours and several microwaved
airport hamburgers after we landed in California, we jumped
on another flight to the island of Kauai, a ridiculously lush
paradise. Most of the homes and hotels were clustered in
a few spots along the coast, and the rest of the land was
blanketed with green trees and rushing with waterfalls.

Our hotel, the Green Room Resort, was spectacular. The
pool was as clear as bottled water. The Wi-Fi was delightful.
And there was a twenty-four-hour ice cream bar with at least
twenty-five different toppings. I practically cried when a
driver picked us up the day after we'd arrived and rushed us
to a nearby airfield, where Ashley Hawking herself was waiting by the underplane.

She didn't really look like a bazillionaire. In my mind,
someone that rich should be a crusty old wrinkled guy who
scowls all the time and has huge unruly gray eyebrows. He
should have a kind of sag or droop to his face, too, as if a
bunch of invisible lead weights are hanging from his cheeks
and jaw. But not Ashley. She was young and fit. She had short,
bright red hair, dark brown eyebrows, thin rectangular glasses,
and some kind of weird dark mole on her left cheek. At first
I thought it was a chocolate donut crumb. I was tempted to
flick it off.

She hurried across the blacktop. "Welcome! Welcome!"

21

she called out. Then she stopped, bit her lip, and squinted. "The leis! I'm so sorry. I forgot the leis."

Hank cupped his hand over his mouth and whispered my way, "The traditional Hawaiian wreath, given during welcomes and farewells."

I knew that.

"Such a shame," she said. "I picked them out myself, too. Steven will be furious. I assured him you'd be greeted properly."

"It's nothing," Hank said. "We're just happy to be here, right, kids?"

We agreed aloud.

"Who's Steven?" I asked.

Ashley didn't answer. "Come, come, we have much to do."

A few minutes later we were up in the air, cruising north over the Pacific Ocean to the tiny island of Nihoa. And now we were down in that ocean, surrounded by water, gliding toward what looked like the world's second-coolest clubhouse. (Sure, I'm a little biased, but Hank's lab still ranked first.) The building was shaped like a pentagon. I'd guess it was about three stories tall and as wide and deep as a basketball court. The middle was all windows, and a huge pipe extended from the left side of the building straight down into the deep blue sea. The pressure was getting to me; I pinched my nose and popped my ears. Then Hank passed us each a piece of gum.

"Is that your house?" Ava asked.

"My lab," Ashley said. "The headquarters of our operation."

The water glowed around the outside. In one of the windows, I thought I saw a kid staring back at us, but then our lights glared off the glass and the mirage was gone. All kinds of fish lurked around the outside, including one long, thick gray creature that made me gasp. "Shark," I muttered.

"Beautiful, isn't she?" Ashley said. "I believe that's Elizabeth."

"Jack's terrified of sharks," Matt explained.

Less so when they're named Elizabeth, but yes, they do frighten me. Is that really so strange?

"Any creature that has managed to survive numerous extinction-level events should be respected," Hank said. "Except maybe for the cockroach. Beautifully engineered, but just so annoying. Is Elizabeth attracted to the lights?"

"She is, yes, and we feed her, too," Ashley said.

"You feed her?" I asked.

The bazillionaire shrugged. "I like sharks."

The underplane nosed toward the bottom of the lab, then glided underneath. As we approached, Ashley throttled back until we slowed almost to a stop. Everyone was quiet. The propellers stopped whirring.

Ava pushed between Matt and me and held her index finger over the touch screen. Eyebrows raised, she looked at Ashley for approval. "We're going up, right?"

"That's right. Go ahead."

Ava tapped the screen. As something hissed below us, she explained, "We're pumping water out of the ballast tanks. Once they're filled with air, the underplane will be buoyant, and we'll start to float up."

Matt pressed his fist to his mouth, then asked, "To the surface?"

"Not yet," Ashley said. "First, the tour."

The underplane rose up through a hole in the bottom of the lab, then burst from the water like a whale breaching for a gulp of air. The vehicle rocked back and forth. My hands were pressed against the back of Ashley's leather seat.

Hank started thinking aloud. "There must be some way to smooth that out. A control system of some kind."

A thin layer of water on my window cleared. I untucked my shirt and wiped away the condensation. We'd popped up in a kind of pool in the middle of a blue and white room with tiled floors.

"A moon pool," Hank remarked. "How clever."

24

"Looks like the deck at the YMCA," Ava said.

My sister was right, except for one thing. "No old people, though," I noted.

The motor purred as Ashley steered the underplane to the edge. A small, goateed man who appeared to be made entirely of muscle reached out, grabbed the underplane by the bow, and pulled it closer. Holding a rope, he signaled Ashley.

"Oh, right," she said. "I forgot." She tapped the touch screen. Something clicked in the front and back of the plane. "Cleats," she said. "So that we can tie up securely, like a normal boat."

"And they're hidden inside so they don't disrupt the aerodynamics in flight," Hank said.

That sounded like something Matt would have noticed, but my brother was still quiet. His eyes were closed, his lips pressed tight.

"Nice touch, Hank," Ava remarked.

Hank scowled. "That wasn't my idea."

"Oh, come on!" Ashley said. "Nobody invents in a vacuum! Well, except maybe that British guy who reinvented the vacuum."

"He didn't reinvent it," Hank muttered. "He merely made it look cooler."

"Who's that?" I asked, pointing to the human-shaped boulder.

"That's Kildare, my SEAL," Ashley said.

"Like Navy SEAL?"

"Yes, everyone in the Valley has one. Once you get a hundred million you basically have to get your own SEAL. He's my bodyguard. Now I'm asking him to take over security down here at the lab, too. Although I'll still come first. I always do."

The underplane stopped rocking. Our doors swung up and open, and we climbed out along the wings and onto the delightfully solid tiled floor. There were puddles of water all around us. I should have warned Matt, but watching him slip and fall would have been nice after such an intense trip, so I kept quiet.

"Thank you, Kildare," Ashley said. "Where's Steven?"

"I believe he's here. He insisted on taking *Luthor* himself."

"Well, it is his boat," Ashley replied. "Don't you think he has that right?"

Kildare didn't answer.

"You can get here by boat, too?" Matt asked.

"Well, yes, I mean, we can't all travel in via underplane, now, can we? There's a dock on the surface, accessible by boat, and stairs from there down to the lab. Does Steven know his guests are here?"

"I believe so," Kildare said.

"Who's Steven?" Ava asked.

Ashley ignored her. "And Rosa?"

"In the control room. She's waiting for you."

"Well then let's go," she said. "Hank?"

Our mentor was crouching beside the underplane with one hand flat on the body. His starry eyes were filled with tears, like a mother gazing proudly upon one of her children.

Matt handed me his computer, and I thought he was going to kneel beside Hank, but then he leaned over the edge of the moon pool. Some kind of monstrous combination of a cough and a burp erupted from his stomach. I backed away. And then it happened. A volcanic explosion from my brother's stomach. He'd been trying to eat more like Hank lately. Salads and greens and all kinds of vegetables. Now, as he dropped to his hands and knees, spewing into the moon pool, the remains of his new diet were floating atop the surface like chopped lilies on a pond. A few little fish kicked to the surface, nibbling at his upchucked lunch.

"Gross," Ava said. "They're eating your—"

"I know," Matt growled.

Hank lifted a hand to his chin. "Fascinating, right? The cycle of life. No wasted nutrients or energy. Are you okay, Matthew?"

My brother held up a hand.

Once his retching slowed down, I crouched close and

27

whispered, "Careful when you get up. There are puddles everywhere."

Hank started to get our bags out of the cargo hold. Ashley insisted that she'd have someone take care of them, and so we just grabbed our backpacks instead. I held Matt's for him and slid his computer inside. But it was heavier than I'd expected. "What's in here?"

Matt started to answer, then unloaded again.

"A telescope, I think," Ava said.

Mine was filled with candy bars. In Antarctica, chocolate and caramel were part of your basic survival kit. So, I figured, why not Hawaii, too? I'd stuffed in a few other random items, but the treats were precious.

A door behind me swung open.

Kildare lifted his left hand, palm facing out, like he had Iron Man–style lasers hiding in there somewhere.

Yet we weren't being attacked.

A boy about my height and age stepped into the room, followed by a tall young woman with buzzed black hair, huge bright eyes, and dark brown skin. Her lips gleamed, and she stared at Ava for a few seconds before turning her radiant smile on Hank. "Dr. Witherspoon? I'm Rosa Morris. I took one of your seminars when you were guest teaching at Caltech a few years—"

He jabbed his index finger in the air, pointing at her. Then he stopped. "Bics!"

"Excuse me?"

"I remember you! Bic pens. You chewed on those cheap plastic pens while you were listening, right?"

She pulled a mangled blue pen out of her pocket. "Still do. They help me concentrate."

"There are worse habits."

"He prefers jazz and sandals," I said.

"What?" Rosa asked.

"Wait, stop," Ashley said. "I'm the host here, yes? Remember? Now, introductions. First and foremost, this is my son, Steven."

The kid in question stared at us like we were no more interesting than a few specks of dust. He was about my height. His blond hair was long and wavy, as if it had been years since his last visit to the barber, and he wore a white T-shirt with a vaguely familiar symbol on the chest, a blue blazer, and black high-top sneakers. His clothes were fine; I had no real problem with them. But there was something about his hair, the arch of one of his eyebrows, and the mathematically straight line formed by his pressed lips that suggested he was going to be difficult.

He'd been holding his hands behind his back, but then he raised one to wave, and in the other I could see that he had a copy of *The Lonely Orphans*. Which was great. Really. Just what I needed, you know? Another devoted fan of the geniuses. Matt and Ava would be thrilled.

29

"Greetings," he said. Then he glanced at me. "Nice bow tie."

I didn't have to be a mind reader to know he didn't mean that. Was it coming loose? I reached up and adjusted the knot.

"Wait," Matt said. He stifled a burp, then continued, "Your name is Steven?"

"Yes."

"So you're named after Stephen Hawking, the famous cosmologist?"

"Mine is spelled with a v," he said.

"Clever, right?" Ashley said. "I knew he'd be smart. His father is a physicist. So I thought I'd anoint him with a suitably noble name. No pressure, though, right Steven?"

Ava pointed to his shirt, which had a graphic of a small dot surrounded by several ellipses. "Nice," she said.

He briefly rocked his head from side to side before replying. "An inaccurate rendition of the atom, created before physicists truly understood uncertainty, but yes, it is nice," Steven answered. He smiled, just barely, at Hank. "I wear it to remind myself that even famed scientists can be wrong."

Ashley turned to the tall woman. "And Hank, Rosa is the ridiculously brilliant lead engineer on the TOES."

I laughed. Steven sighed. My siblings wouldn't look at me. "What?" I asked. "She said toes."

"Which is short for Thermal Ocean Energy System," Ava reminded me.

Right. That was the whole reason we were there in the first place.

"Anyway," Ashley continued, "I found her toiling—"

"You didn't find me."

"Discovered?"

"No," Rosa said, "we met . . ." Now she stopped and smiled at Ava. "What's up?" she asked. Ava stammered and looked away. "Tell me," Rosa said. "What's on your mind?"

"Hank didn't tell me you were . . ."

"Black?"

Hank shrugged. "Sorry, I didn't think it was important."

"It isn't," Rosa said. "But then it is, right, Ava? It means everything and nothing at once."

My sister opened her mouth to reply but said nothing.

After an uncomfortably long pause, Ashley clapped. "So serious! Yikes. Anyway, Steven is turning thirteen in two days. Steven, meet your new friends, Matthew, Ava, and . . ."

She was staring at me. "Jack," Matt answered for me.

"Right."

The four of us stood awkwardly for what felt like an eternity. Matt started looking up at the ceiling. Ava was nodding, as if to some beat playing only in her head. After holding eye contact with Steven for far too long, I

31

stared down at my high-tops. They were new—I'd found them in Hank's lab, stuffed underneath a bench packed with random inventions. He'd let us know that we could borrow anything on that table, and these had fit perfectly. But there were already some creases in the leather. A drop of water had seeped in and begun to spread. I studied it as closely as I could, but you can really only stare at your shoes for so long. At some point I was going to have to look up again.

"Well!" Ashley said at last. "Let's go talk about the TOES, shall we?"

I laughed again. Hank glared at me.

"That sounds perfect," Matt said.

Hank followed Rosa through a door into a brightly lit stairwell. They were chattering away, their shoes clanging on the metal, when Ashley stopped on the first step and turned around. "Oh, dear, I'm sorry. Not you three."

"Not us?" Matt asked. He leaned to the right, trying to look up the stairs. "Hank?"

"You'll see him again shortly," Ashley answered. "First I need to borrow his brain. This is serious work, kids. Steven, why don't you tell your new friends about some of the things you've been working on? The nuclear reactor might interest them. Or maybe they're hungry? Yes, they look hungry. I'll have Kildare bring down some sandwiches. Have fun.

Enjoy. I'm so happy to see the three of you together. And you, too, Jake."

The door clanked shut. Steven laughed quietly. He still held the book at his side.

"Jack," I mumbled.

Matt watched the door, as if the bazillionaire was going to pop back through at any second and say she was joking. "I don't get it," he said.

"Neither do I," Ava added. "She's treating us like—"

"Children?" Steven said.

"Exactly."

In a slow, precise tone, Steven said, "Just so we're clear, I don't want to be here, either. But if we have to spend time together we may as well be productive." He rapped the cover of *The Lonely Orphans* with his knuckles.

"Did you really build a nuclear reactor?" Ava asked. "Any chance we could have a look?"

"By Newton's apple, no!" Steven responded. "I'm not going to show you my intellectual property. You'd probably steal it and pass it off as your own. And I highly doubt you'll be able to teach me anything, anyway. But if you ever need funding, I have a few million dollars set aside for investments. I'd be happy to consider one of your inventions. In the meantime, though, I think we'll all be better off if I do the teaching. Here, take this," he said, handing Ava the book.

33

Lights were flashing in my head. Fireworks, really. Before my sister could say anything, I interrupted. "Did you say you have a few million dollars?"

He made a clicking noise with his tongue. "It's a start."

I almost fainted. Our poetry book had sold well. I considered us rich. For kids, anyway. But millions? That was a whole different solar system. Suddenly Steven didn't seem so terrible. Sure, he was arrogant. Maybe a little annoying. His hair bothered me. But he was rich. Wonderfully, fabulously wealthy. Surely that counted for something.

With a bright smile, Ava asked, "Do you want us to write anything special?"

Steven chuckled. "No, I don't want your autograph!" He paused to laugh again, but this second round was forced.

"What's so funny?" Matt asked. He grabbed his backpack from me and slipped it over his shoulders.

"If you flip through the book you'll see that I've made a number of corrections. These poems . . . a few have potential, I think, but even those are really just first drafts." He stopped at a page near the middle. "This one here, for example. You write, 'We carry our hearts in a shoebox / We fill it with all of our dreams / From home to home it travels—' "

"'Always bursting at the seams,'" Matt said, finishing for him.

"Right, yes. I was wondering how you'd read that last line, as there does seem to be a rhythmic glitch, but that's not my main concern."

"No? What's your main concern?" Ava asked. There was a flash of fire in her voice.

"Word choice," Steven replied. He paused and tugged at his right earlobe, then continued. "Your choice of *home* here is decent, but I think if you'd used the word *house*, you'd have more impact. These weren't your homes, after all. They were merely houses. Places you were forced to live."

Ava pressed her thumb to the tip of her tongue and started turning the pages. "Wait," she said, "you corrected the whole thing?"

"You don't have to thank me," he said. "Read away."

While Ava was staring down at the marked pages, Matt was eyeing the door again. "But I thought we were here to help," he said.

"You thought what?" Steven asked.

"We're here to help Hank figure out what's wrong with the power plant. We're here to fix the TOES." He looked from Steven to Ava to me. "Right?"

Steven laughed through his nose. Thankfully nothing came out. Then he slapped his knee. Twice. Really—who does that? Suddenly the millions didn't feel so important,

BILL NYE and GREGORY MONE

and I was overwhelmed by a desire to prank him. But how? Lunch might offer a chance. I could find a bathroom, pocket some toilet paper, then slip a small square below the top slice of bread in his sandwich when he wasn't looking. Right below the cheese.

"I don't get it," Ava said. "What's so funny?"

"You're not here to help them," Steven said.

"We're not?"

"No, no, no," he said. "Ashley is hosting a birthday party for me on Wednesday night. You three are here to be my friends."

36

3

WE'RE NOT
ENTERTAINMENT

CREEPY? YES, A LITTLE. AND I COULD SEE HOW YOU might think it was sad, too. The kid's mom had flown in strangers for his birthday party. You can almost imagine her going through the party-planning list in her head. Let's see. Piñata? Check. Chips? Check. Soda? Check. Kids? No!

Sure, he was lonely. Isolated. Friendless. But he was also a millionaire! And if you were to spend any time with Steven Hawking, every last drop of your sympathy would evaporate. The kid was more annoying than a housefly and as arrogant as a pop star. We were the ones who deserved sympathy. We were the ones who'd been duped.

Ava and Matt thought they'd been brought in to help fix a potentially world-changing technology. I thought we were going to get a chance to solve another mystery.

Now it turned out that we'd made the trip just for a birthday party. Or that's what Steven and his mother had planned, anyway. But I was already plotting a way to steer us in a different direction, and I didn't need to talk to my siblings to know they'd follow. We were going to find Hank and mop up this mess as soon as possible.

As I silently schemed, and Matt took a turn scanning the pages of *The Lonely Orphans*, Steven started tapping his foot impatiently. Finally, he shouted, "Where are those sandwiches?" He stomped out of the room through a green door. "I'll be right back," he said. "Wait here."

We did not. The second he was gone we dashed to the other door and the stairwell. Ava led the way, and Matt tossed the book across the room like a Frisbee. *The Lonely Orphans* landed with a slap, spun through a puddle, and just missed sliding over the edge into the water. I stopped. This was an amazing opportunity. A chance to see the geniuses corrected? I couldn't just leave that lying on the floor. I had to have that copy. Maybe I could even read the revised poems aloud at night, to annoy them before bed. I rushed back, grabbed the book, and stuffed it below my shirt, under the waistband at the back of my pants.

"Are you coming?" Matt called. "Or are you waiting for Steven?"

I darted up the stairs.

A woman's voice said, "Keep going!"

I stopped and looked down, then up. The three of us

were alone in the stairwell. But I'd definitely heard someone. And she sounded British. "Did anyone else hear that?"

"Hear what?" Ava asked.

The door to the floor above us swung open and banged against the wall. Hank emerged, and when he spotted us he held his hands up and his head back. "I was just coming for you, honestly."

"We didn't come here as entertainment," Matt said. He wiped his mouth with his forearm.

"This was not my idea," Hank swore. "I didn't even know she had a boy."

"He's not a boy," Ava said. "He's a demon."

I held up *The Lonely Orphans*. "They're mad because he corrected their poetry."

"That's what you went back for, Jack?" Matt asked. "Are you serious?"

"Come on, come on," Hank said. "Ashley went to the bathroom, so I hurried to grab you."

Hank led us into a large circular room. The curved walls were inset with windows looking out into the sea. A massive, slick shark kicked through a school of silvery blue fish. I stepped back. "Elizabeth again?"

"She's not going to bite you," Matt said.

A door in the wall opened slightly. "Who's that?" asked Ashley. "Steven?"

Rosa, the engineer, held her hand to her forehead, then pointed to the door. "She's in the bathroom," Rosa mouthed. Then, to Ashley, she answered, "Just Hank and the kids. Don't worry, we'll wait for you to get started."

Now Rosa moved over to the window and pointed to the shark. "That might be Wanda. I don't see them now, but there are others. Ron, Frank, and a few I forget. Ashley had all the sharks tagged with tracking devices, then created a little app that talks to the tags, so we know where they are at all times." She pointed to a screen behind me showing a map of the island, the lab, and the surrounding seas. Small red dots moved around in the water. "But enough about the sharks. Take a look at this," she said, pointing to the large table in the center of the room. A five-foot-tall model of the TOES and its surroundings was encased in a Plexiglass box in the middle of the table. Near the top, a layer of deep blue plastic sheeting stretched across the walls of the cube. There was a dock at the surface, and a clear tube extending diagonally down to a miniature version of the underwater lab. From there, a long, thin pipe extended down to the ocean floor. And how did I know this was the bottom? Because someone had placed a small figurine of a famous cartoon sponge down there, next to the base of the pipe.

Now, before I say what I'm going to say next, let it be clear that I don't play with action figures anymore. Got it? Good. But if I were still interested in that sort of stuff, I could see setting up a few guys on the dock, then maybe stationing a few down at the bottom, next to the poorly dressed sponge, and having them battle. G.I. Joe figures would be perfect, but I could see mixing in some other toys. Aquaman, maybe. The pipe could be a kind of slide. Or not. As I said, I'm not really into playing with toys.

"We had this built for the big ceremony last month," Rosa said. "We thought it would help people understand how the TOES works."

Hank crouched in front of the display. Naturally, Matt did the exact same thing a few feet away, and Ava circled the model, squinting.

Ashley's muffled response came out from behind the bathroom door. "And it did help them!"

Hank eyed the three of us in turn. He didn't say anything, but based on his dramatically raised left eyebrow, I could guess his meaning. Hank was very serious about manners. He was correcting our chewing habits all the time, and now he was trying to let us know that contributing to a conversation while you were attending to personal business

41

on the other side of a closed bathroom door was on the list of forbidden behaviors.

"But then the system failed when we switched it on," Rosa added.

Hank stood up; his knees cracked. "What went wrong?" he asked.

"That's what we're trying to figure out," Rosa said.

Now Matt moved next to Ava, who was leaning forward, studying the base of the pipe. "How does it work?" she asked. "What's the pipe for?"

Rosa glanced over at Hank. "Go ahead," he said.

"Right. Well, I was just explaining it to Hank here. So let me see . . . what's the problem with electricity?"

"We don't have enough of it," I blurted out.

"No."

That would be the last time I'd speak for a while.

"We need a more efficient way of making it," Ava said.

"I prefer the word *generating*, but yes, that's the basic idea. Why?"

Matt held out his hand, silently asking Ava for a turn. She nodded. "Because the standard method is to burn fossil fuels like oil, which pumps carbon dioxide into the atmosphere," he said.

Ava jumped in again quickly. "And that traps heat near the surface, forcing Earth to warm."

Hank beamed proudly at his two prized students.

"Good, good," Rosa said.

"A little simplistic, though, right?" Matt said. "There's more to it than that."

"Is there? Really?" Rosa asked. "To me it is a fairly simple system. Pumping heat-trapping gasses into the air is like leaving the windows closed in your car in the middle of summer. It gets hot inside."

"Sure, if you look at the globe like an engineer, but—"

"But what?" Rosa asked.

Matt's face reddened, and Ava was really struggling to hide her smile. My brother glanced at Hank, but our mentor shrugged. The argument was Matt's to win or lose.

The toilet flushed. Ashley stepped out of the bathroom a second later. There was no way she had time to wash her hands. Maybe she washed them first, then used the kick-flush move? No. We would've heard the faucet.

"Beautiful, isn't it?" Ashley asked, pointing to the model.

Rosa was still awaiting my brother's response. In an attempt to save Matt, I asked what I guessed was a dumb question. "So do you get the electricity off the sea floor or something?"

"That's a dumb question," Matt said.

Thanks, bud.

With a smile, Ashley added, "Where would you find electricity in the ocean?"

43

BILL NYE and GREGORY MONE

"Electric eels?" I suggested. Then I spread my arms out wide. "Really, really big ones."

They all laughed hysterically. At me, I guess. But what if you could do that? What if you had some kind of underwater charging station, and the eels swam up to it, blasted a few volts into the machine, and then swam away? You could feed them fish or something to encourage them to keep coming back, the way Ashley did with the sharks.

I clamped my head with my hands. What was wrong with me? Hanging around with the geniuses all the time was twisting my brain in knots. Now I was starting to get ideas, too. Only mine were all backward and upside down.

Matt lightly kicked the side of my foot. Apparently Rosa had already started explaining. "So once we pump this really cold water up the pipe from the sea floor, it cools the superheated steam. That way the fluid can be used again. The result is a beautiful low-emissions process."

She paused. Hank was staring at a desk chair, and he looked like his mind was on another planet entirely. But my siblings were clearly following her. I held up my hand. "Sorry, I missed the part about the . . . everything."

Looking at Rosa, Ava explained, "Basically, the TOES uses warm water from the ocean surface to heat up this fluid and turn it into steam. The steam then spins a turbine, which makes electricity."

She turned to me, checking to make sure I understood. I nodded. "Okay."

Now Matt jumped in. "Then the TOES uses the really cold water from the deep ocean to cool the steam and turn it back into a liquid, starting the process over again."

"The system harvests wave energy, too," Ava added. "Rosa's the first one to think of that."

Matt held up his index finger like a professor. "And it doesn't pump any smog or carbon dioxide into the air."

"Which means it doesn't contribute to global warming," Ava finished.

Rosa nodded to Hank. "They really are bright."

His eyebrows did a little dance. Mentally, he had rejoined us. "I know, right?"

Obviously they weren't talking about me. I was still confused. "What do you mean it 'harvests' wave energy?"

"Kind of like farmers harvesting potatoes," Matt explained. "They take the food out of the ground. The TOES captures energy from the waves and the difference between the warm and cold water, too."

"Exactly!" Rosa said.

My siblings were shining so brightly I was getting a sunburn. Were they going to multiply large numbers next? Juggle?

"It didn't take Steven long to figure out, either," Ashley

added. "I believe he even had a few tips for improving the efficiency, didn't he, Rosa?"

"No," she responded flatly. "This design is entirely—"

"By the way," Ashley said, cutting her off, "where is Steven?" She leaned to one side, then the other, studying me as if I were hiding him somewhere. Did she think he was in my back pocket?

The door crashed open. The little longhaired prince stood there scowling and holding a tray. Kildare was behind him.

"Steven dear, we were just—"

He held up a slice of wheat bread from one of the sandwiches. The backside was smeared with mayonnaise. "Seriously? Do you even see this? How many times do we have to tell them? Gluten free means gluten free."

Ashley sighed sympathetically. "I'll fire them all, I promise. Each and every one."

"After the party," Steven said. "We do need them for the party."

"Right, yes. After the party."

Were these two serious? I glanced at Ava to see if she was wondering the same thing, but she was focused on the model.

Steven dropped the sandwich onto the tray, then passed it back to Kildare. "Have the Little Einsteins discovered the glitch yet, Rosa?"

"You can call me Dr. Morris."

Hank shuffled over to the ex-SEAL and grabbed one of the sandwiches. "We haven't gotten to the glitch yet," he said, chomping off a huge bite. At first he looked pleased. Then he winced and swallowed painfully. "What is this?"

"Vegan ham and almond cheese," Kildare said.

"On wheat bread," Steven added with annoyance.

"Tastes like wet sand," Hank said. He grabbed a glass off the table and swigged. Then he coughed and choked briefly. "What was that?"

"Pure cauliflower juice," Ashley said. "It's so, so healthy and cleansing."

Hank glared at me. "Stop smiling, Jake."

That was low.

"Shouldn't you kids be doing something else?" Ashley asked. "How about a game of prime factors?"

"You don't mind if we listen instead, do you?" Matt said.

"Please?" Ava asked.

"They won't be a bother," Hank assured her.

Reluctantly, Ashley agreed.

The rest of them started talking about the TOES and the temperature of the ocean again, but my thoughts drifted as quickly as a spacewalking astronaut cut loose from his tether. First I returned to the ice cream bar at the hotel on Kauai. But before long I was thinking about those eels

47

again. What if you could breed a whole bunch and keep them inside small tanks under the hoods of cars to power the batteries? Maybe I could get Steven to give me the money for a test experiment. If it worked, people wouldn't need gasoline engines anymore. Everything would run on eels. That would certainly make for exciting car accidents.

When I returned from my mind-drift, they were discussing the possible flaws with the TOES. The geniuses move fast, and I hadn't interrupted them in a while, so I raised my hand.

"This isn't kindergarten," Steven said.

"It's a habit," Ava explained.

And it worked. So there. Unfortunately, though, I didn't really have a question. "Just so I'm clear, what you're saying is . . ." I trailed off, letting my last word hang in the air like a tossed football, waiting for someone to catch it and run.

Ava saved me. "She's saying that the TOES is using more electricity than it produces."

"Since the demonstration," Rosa added. "Before that, the system worked beautifully."

"But it's broken now, Rosa," Steven added.

"Dr. Morris," Rosa snapped.

"So who did it?" I asked.

"Who did what?" Ashley asked.

I pointed to Steven. "He said it's broken. So who broke it?"

"Well that's an odd question!" Ashley replied. "We don't know that it was broken by someone. It could have just . . . broken."

I didn't like her answer. Or the way her eyes flitted between Hank and Rosa and Kildare. Or how she shifted her weight from one foot to the other as if she were rocking to some secret dance beat.

Rosa pointed a partially chewed Bic pen in my direction. "So you think it could've been sabotage, huh?"

Before I could reply, Ava tapped on the Plexiglass case. "Do you know where all the waste is going? If it's using more electricity than it's producing, then we should figure out where the system is breaking down. Right?"

If I had a spitball, I would've launched it at Ava's head.

"Yes, yes," Ashley said. "That's exactly how we were thinking about it. To get all that cold water up to the surface, you need a pump, and it looks like the pump is working a lot harder than it was before."

"And if it's working harder, it's using more electricity," Matt explained.

Hank made a clicking noise with his tongue and pointed at Ashley. "That's why you wanted me to send the *Nautilus Redux*. You want to go down there, don't you?"

Ava brightened. "Hank, you brought your submarine?"

Kildare stepped forward, still holding the tray of

49

sandwiches. "Ashley?"

The bazillionaire ignored him. Her eyelids fluttered as she looked at Hank. She bit her lower lip. "What if we just take a quick look?"

"I thought we were just going to do a little pleasure cruising," Hank said. He kneeled before the model, eyeing the sponge at the bottom. "I've never taken her deeper than twenty feet."

"In a tank," Ava said.

"But at the conference in San Jose last year you told me she could withstand pressure to depths of three thousand feet."

"Sure, according to all my calculations that should hold true, but . . ."

"What about the underplane?" I asked.

I just wanted to say "underplane" again.

"Ashley?"

"Kildare! I do not want a sandwich. Please stop forcing them on me!"

"It's not about the sandwiches," the bodyguard replied. "Those islanders are back. They're doing some kind of ceremony right above us."

To my surprise, Ashley Hawking stuck out her tongue, dropped her muscly shoulders, sagged forward, and let out the slowest, most dramatically pronounced fake puking noise I've ever heard. Then she swept her hand across her face and transformed, plastering on a welcoming smile. "Well then, we might as well go say hello. We have plenty of time to talk about the *Nautilus Redux*, and I suspect you'll all find this little experience, and these people, interesting."

Hank nodded to Ava and Matt, then me. "Could be a chance to learn something, guys. Everyone you meet knows something you don't."

Matt clapped once with excitement. "Let's go then."

Rosa chose to remain behind at the lab, but the rest of us followed Kildare. He swung a huge backpack with two swim fins sticking out the top over his shoulders, then led the way out of the room and into an enclosed stairwell that extended up through twenty feet of water to the platform on the surface. Giant windows lined the sides. A school of silvery fish the size of Magic Markers hovered within arm's reach. One of the sharks was gliding slowly back and forth in the distance. I pressed my hand to the glass; it was cool but not cold.

At the top, Ashley opened the door to the floating platform and we stepped outside. The water was still and calm, and the old wooden sailing vessels were a few city blocks away. Two inflatable powerboats as long as station wagons, with engines the size of washing machines, were tied up to the dock. I drooled.

"The one on the left, *Luthor*, is mine," Steven boasted. "The other one is *Vader*."

Hank chuckled. To Ashley, he added, "Why villains?"

"Heroes are boring," she replied. "Villains are so much more intriguing."

Matt tapped my elbow. "Who's Luthor?"

Moments like that? I lived for them. And while I could've run around the dock singing *I know something you don't know*, I answered quickly instead, explaining that the villain in question was the nemesis of Superman and a rare and brilliant criminal mind.

Besides, I was more concerned with Ashley than teasing my brother. So she preferred villains. Did that mean she was one herself? Had she sabotaged the TOES? And if so, why?

"Don't stop now. Keep going!" a woman said.

That voice again! The same one I'd heard in the stairwell, back in the lab. The accent was definitely British. But where was it coming from? Ava was looking at me. "You heard that, right?" I asked.

"Yeah, but it wasn't me," she said. "Come on, let's go."

"Who are those people?" Matt asked, pointing at the wooden boats.

Ashley explained that the visitors were native Hawaiians

from nearby Kauai. They believed Nihoa was a sacred piece of Hawaiian history and tradition and that the TOES should not have been built in or around its waters. Ashley's argument was that the health of our planet was more important than the cultural history of a large rock. Plus, she said she'd already secured the rights to build there. "They're fighting a battle that's been over for two years," she said. "But remember your Sun Tzu, Steven. Your enemies are your friends and your friends are your enemies."

Kildare tossed his pack into *Vader*. "That's not exactly right," he muttered.

"What was that?" Ashley asked.

"Nothing," he replied.

"Good, I thought so."

I leaned to Matt and whispered, "What was that all about? She mentioned that Sun guy again."

"Sun Tzu was an ancient Chinese philosopher," Matt said. "He wrote a really famous book on military strategy called *The Art of War*."

"Are we at war?" I asked.

Matt stopped. "I don't think so," he said. "But if her friends are her enemies and her enemies are her friends, I'm not really sure where that leaves us."

53

4

HE WHO BATHES
BENEATH WATERFALLS

WE CLIMBED INTO *VADER*, AND THE WATER WAS
so still and clear and beautiful that I might
have jumped in if I hadn't seen those sharks. I
probably would've been fine, but once you've
seen a shark in the water, that ferocious beast is everywhere,
lurking in every drop, waiting to chomp off your foot for a
crunchy afternoon snack.

Hank stood at the back, next to Ashley, and the rest of us
moved to the bow. There were cushioned seats, but we were
all too excited to sit. Kildare lifted one up and motioned for
us to stow our backpacks inside. Then he turned to Steven.
"Did you leave your keys? Rosa will need a way back."

Steven sighed heavily, climbed out of the boat, and stuck
the keys to *Luthor* in the ignition. "If she does anything to it,
I'm blaming you."

"Ready?" Ashley called out. Before anyone could answer,

she pushed forward on the throttle. The boat screamed away from the dock, churning whitewater in its wake.

The larger of the two wooden boats was built of two canoes as long as city buses, joined by a wide rectangular platform. A polished and stained wooden mast stood near the bow. Near the stern, a long black paddle reached into the water between the canoes. The platform stretched the length of each hull, and a few men and women stood at the edge of the one closest to us, tossing flower petals into the sea. The pink flowers spread out on the surface, moving with the current.

The second boat was a miniature version of the first, but only about the length and width of a large SUV. It clung to the back of the larger craft by a long, slack rope, and a kid stood at the helm. The sun was behind her, outlining her in gold, and her long black hair was swept up in a side pony-tail. She wore sunglasses, a Lakers jersey, board shorts, and no shoes. Ava shoved my seat from behind. She may have caught me staring.

Vader slowed. The engine was quiet enough that we could hear ourselves talk. "The whole protecting the history of the island thing is just one piece, by the way," Ashley said. "They're also playing the environmental card."

"What do you mean?" Hank asked.

55

"They claim that we're a risk to the Nihoa finch, an endangered species of bird found only on this island," Ashley explained. "But it's just a little mouse with wings. Some species are better off disappearing, you know?"

"Uh . . . I . . ." Hank stuttered. He was so shocked he couldn't even speak.

"They're surfers, too, and in the right conditions, Nihoa gets some of the best waves in the islands," Ashley added. "They've been complaining that the TOES disrupts the waves, since it's right offshore. But I don't even think any of those are the real reason for their protest."

Steven started to say something, then stopped. My brother, meanwhile, was holding his hand over his mouth. Was he going to upchuck again? I hoped not. Sure, it would be kind of funny, but not if his vomit stuck to the boat.

"So what's the real reason?" Ava asked.

"Jealousy," Ashley said. "They're jealous that I'm living here. It's only supposed to be temporary, of course. But I don't have any intention of leaving. Not for a few years, anyway. Either way, they're here, they're annoying, and I have to find a way to get rid of them without causing a massive public-relations mess." She pointed to the side of the larger boat. "Take the wheel, Hank, and pull up alongside."

As Hank steered us closer, Ashley readied the lines. She brushed past me to grab a rope, and her body odor flooded my nose. It wasn't terrible, exactly. Just unexpected. She smelled like men's underarm deodorant. A particular brand, in fact. The scent reminded me of the owner of the German deli across the street from Hank's lab. Suddenly I wanted a ham sandwich with mustard.

Leaning against the side, line in hand, Ashley studied me. "Are you hungry, Jack? You should've had some lunch."

She got my name right this time. So she'd either learned from her mistake or she knew it all along. In that case, she was now being nice. Which meant I was her enemy. Or her friend?

My brain was a big, hardened knot.

"Wave with me," Ashley said. "Wave and smile."

The islanders stopped throwing flowers. Four of them stood on the long platform. The man in the center of the group had broad shoulders, bronze skin, full red lips, and dark eyebrows as thick as his short black hair. He wore red board shorts and a necklace made of small shells. He looked like the kind of guy who went days without wearing a shirt. A small, thin, and equally bronzed old man with bright white hair and a huge black watch stood to his right, back a step. A tall woman loomed behind him, and next to her a tattooed and fierce-looking guy was scowling at us. They all looked as if they'd been plucked out of a coral reef somewhere, not born and bred on dry land like normal humans.

Out of the side of her mouth, while she was waving,

Ashley asked, "Can you spot the leader? Don't give them any clues, Steven."

The leader? I wanted to pick out which one might be a criminal mastermind, a man or woman with the cunning and drive to take down a thirty-million-dollar experiment. But the old man looked too, well, old. The guy with the tattoos all across his shoulders seemed like a good suspect. Then I focused. The tattoo on his left shoulder was a perfect picture of Ariel, the mermaid princess with the beautiful singing voice. Did brilliant crooks get princess tattoos?

"Come on," Ashley repeated, "guess."

"The guy with the necklace?" I asked.

"No, but he wants to be," Ava said. "I'd say the older dude in the back."

"Ding!" Ashley replied, sounding way too much like a computer. "A real leader doesn't need to be out front and center."

As the man with the necklace crossed his arms on his broad chest, Matt noted, "They don't seem happy to see us."

"Do they speak English?" I asked.

Ashley looked at me like I'd just broken the world record for stupidest comment. "My friends!" she called out. "So nice to see you!"

"We were performing a ceremony," the man with the necklace answered. "We're not going to leave. We have a right to be here."

"That's David," Ashley said to us. Then, to him, she continued, "I wasn't going to ask you to leave! As you know, you're welcome to camp on my beach."

"It's not your beach. And we were already planning to camp there. We don't need your invitation."

Ashley laughed. "Technicalities! Anyway, I'd like to invite you all to a party tomorrow night. No. What's today? Monday? The party is Wednesday night."

Angrily, Steven whispered, "Ashley! How could you?"

She turned and mouthed, "They won't come." Then she faced the islanders again. "Can we help with your ceremony?"

"No," David answered.

The old man placed a hand on David's shoulder and edged forward. "Who are the kids?" he asked.

"Friends of Steven's."

I glanced at Ava. Since when were we his friends?

"And behind the wheel?"

"An associate of mine."

"You might as well come aboard," David said with a shrug.

The woman tossed Ashley a rope, which she looped around one of the cleats. Steven crawled to the stern and tied up a second line. His balance was impressive. He jumped around like a cat.

One at a time, we climbed onto the boat. The old man

59

was standing on a low platform. He curled his tanned toes over the edge and crouched. He held the side of his hand flat against his brow and squinted at Hank. Then he smiled, revealing two rows of ridiculously bright white teeth. The glare of those chompers was blinding. I almost needed sunglasses. And they just didn't match with the rest of him. His deep wrinkles and matted hair suggested he wouldn't have any teeth at all.

In a sandpaper-rough voice, he asked, "Is that Henry Witherspoon?"

Hank hopped out. "It is! I am. But call me Hank, please."

"Your nose vacuum saved my life!"

"Really?"

We were crowded along the side, unsure of where to go. Matt nudged me out of the way, stepping carefully toward the large central platform in the middle of the boat so he could be closer to Hank.

"Well, not saved, exactly, but improved. It is wonderful. We all have one." The tall, thin woman produced one of the sleek silver contraptions from a pack wrapped around her waist. The nose vacuum—a mucous and booger extractor that's probably Hank's greatest contribution to the world—gleamed in the sunlight. "Come! Come!" the old man said, waving us forward. "Please, please, let us show you *Ohana*. This boat represents our history! Have you ever seen a star compass?"

Ava was squinting. "*Ohana* . . . that means family, right?"

"Indeed!" the old man replied.

"You speak Hawaiian?" asked the man with the mermaid tattoo. His voice was surprisingly high-pitched, almost squeaky. This was disappointing. I wanted it to be deep. Growling. You know, villainous.

"She speaks everything," I said.

"Yes, well, no offense to your nose vacuum, Hank," the old man said, "but this vessel you're standing on now is real technology."

"Yeah, about a thousand years ago," Steven quipped.

"Four thousand, actually," Ashley said. "Isn't that right, David?"

David looked like he didn't want to speak another word to us. A nudge from the old man encouraged him. "Yes, that's right. This is an exact re-creation of the boats the ancient Polynesians used to cross the Pacific and populate all these islands."

"So it's a replica?" Matt asked.

"More like a modern fabrication of an ancient design," Hank said. "It reminds me of the *Kon-Tiki*."

David spat. The guy with the mermaid tattoo stared down at the spittle on the deck, and the old man responded with unexpected fire in his voice. "That raft was an abomination! Why everyone believed a man named after a Norse god could

61

tell the world about Polynesian culture I will never know. That was fake! This is real." He flicked his head in the direction of the smaller boat, where the girl was sitting cross-legged, watching us. "And my granddaughter's boat, *Niu*, will be just as well made." Then he asked Ava, "Do you know what the name means?"

Her left eye was half closed as she guessed, "Large, right? Grand?"

"No, that's *n-u-i*," the old man answered with a smile. "*Niu* means 'coconut.' "

"Why coconut?" I asked. Because it was funny?

David replied, "She thought it was funny."

Already I liked this girl. I pointed to Ava. "My sister named a toaster Bob."

"Yes, well, all names aside, my granddaughter's boat will be a work of wonder. She's building it herself."

"She's building that herself? Amazing!" Hank said.

"Whatever," Ava grumbled. "It's just wood. You don't even have to write any software."

"The world does not run on code alone, young lady," the old man replied.

"It will soon," Ashley quipped.

Matt held up his index finger. He was probably ready to spout some theory about how the universe really was just a big computer program. I gave him a subtle "not-now" shake of the head. Surprisingly, he kept his mouth closed, and we all introduced ourselves. The old man's name was Ben. This was mildly disappointing. I'd been hoping he was going to have some kind of cool island name, like Ko'ono or Makapaka. Something that had meaning. He who bathes beneath waterfalls, maybe. Or the one who tiptoes across the waves.

The others had similarly disappointing names. The woman was Betsy. I mean, really. Betsy? What kind of Hawaiian name was that? And the tattooed guy was Derek. Ever heard of a surfing saboteur named Derek? Nope. Me neither. Plus, the mermaid wasn't the only princess art on his back. He had the whole lineup, from Cinderella to Snow White. As for the rest of the crew, the girl's name was Maya, and Ben said she was his granddaughter. David was his son.

"Are you all Hawaiian?" Hank asked.

"No, I'm from Jersey," Derek said. "Everyone else is the real deal, though."

As they showed us around the boat, Ben noticed that Matt didn't look quite right. He handed him a pack of gum; he said chewing it would settle his stomach. Then Ben told us that he'd only become interested in his heritage in the last two decades. Before that he was a very devoted and successful dentist. "Now David runs the practice," he explained.

63

Again he flashed his teeth. The glare was even more startling up close. "We specialize in whitening."

Hank pointed to Ben's watch. "That, sir, is a beauty. Are you a SCUBA diver?"

David put his hand on the old man's shoulder. "He doesn't need tanks. He's one of the best free divers in the islands."

"Used to be," Ben said.

"Senseless sport," Steven said. "Unnecessarily dangerous. People die all the time."

"Yes, but only if they fail to respect the water," Betsy chimed in. "We're not like that."

"Blah, blah, blah," Steven replied.

Ashley said nothing. Weren't parents supposed to, you know, parent at moments like that, when their kids were being rude and disrespectful? I wouldn't know. But her barely hidden smile suggested she was proud.

Ben ignored the brat. "Come, come. Hank, my friend, let me show you something," he said, waving to a large, square canvas mat rolled out in the middle of the platform. There was an enormous circle in the middle with markings along the circumference and parallel lines connecting the dots on either side, like the latitude lines on a globe.

"Is this a star compass?" Hank asked.

"Indeed it is."

"Cute, isn't it?" Ashley said aloud.

Hank frantically summoned Matt, and my brother looked like he'd just been given front-row seats to a Knicks game. Actually, scratch that. He wouldn't care about such prime tickets. Anyway, our mentor was instantly obsessed, and while Matt was excited at first, the map clearly confused him. Normally, he studied the stars through a computer screen, not on a canvas mat. As Ben explained how it worked, the two of them huddled around the star compass with Ashley, Steven, and the others.

Ava and I stood at the back of the crowd, and my brain started drifting again. Sure, they'd all laughed, but I still liked that eel idea. What if you had the electric eels powering your home, too? Maybe you could hook them up to your security system, so that when burglars tried to break in, they'd get a shock.

"They're not buying it, you know."

Behind us, Maya, the girl in the Lakers shirt, was sitting cross-legged on a furled-up canvas sail.

"Buying what?" I asked in a low voice.

"Pele's story."

"The soccer player?"

"No, the Hawaiian fire goddess," Ava said. Honestly, how did she know this stuff? She pointed her thumb at Ashley. "You call her Pele? That's funny."

65

"It's the red hair, mostly, but she is pretty fiery."

I pointed to her shirt. Finally I'd have something to talk about. "You're a Lakers fan? Who's your favorite player?"

"What?" She looked down at her jersey. "Oh, right. I don't really know basketball. This was in a hotel lost and found, and I like purple."

My mood sank like an anchor.

"Jack wants to be in the NBA," Ava said. And it wasn't entirely untrue. That was one of the possible futures I'd outlined for myself, along with becoming the leader of a small, wealthy, peaceful nation. One with wide beaches, tall forests, and universal Wi-Fi. Lately I'd been thinking more about becoming a rock star, too. But the whole musical talent thing was going to be tricky. I'd never picked up an instrument, and the few times I'd sung in front of people, they thought I was joking.

"You're a good basketball player?" Maya asked.

"He doesn't even practice."

This may have been true, but I wasn't letting it dampen my dreams. "My natural ability will emerge soon," I said.

She held up her hand, a motionless wave to Ava. "I'm Maya," she said.

"Your grandfather told us," Ava said. Then my sister introduced us. I stepped forward to shake Maya's hand. And as I saw my hand out there, moving toward her through the air, I realized it was a mistake. Kids my age don't shake. And boys definitely don't shake hands with strange new girls. But my hand was moving ahead like a spaceship with no landing dock in sight.

Maya offered me the motionless wave. I retracted my hand and did the same.

"That wasn't awkward at all," Ava said.

Thanks, sis.

I jammed my hands in my pockets, never wanting to see either one of them ever again. Then I nodded toward Ben. "That's your grandfather?"

"He already told us that," Ava said.

Thanks again.

"Yes, and my uncle David," Maya explained.

"I thought he was your dad," I said.

"No, my parents aren't into all this cultural heritage stuff. But they travel for work all the time, so they let me hang out with my grandfather and my uncle." She glanced back and forth between my sister and me. "So, you two are related?"

Ava had introduced me as her brother. I could see how that might be confusing. "Sort of," I replied. "See, we used to—"

"What's their problem with the TOES?" my sister demanded, cutting me off. "The waves? The birds?"

"Well, first of all," Maya replied, "no one should even be here. This is supposed to be a historical and cultural preserve, but somehow she got a pass."

"And second?" Ava pressed.

"The thing doesn't even work!" Maya protested.

"It did work," I noted.

"But the demonstration was a huge failure."

"Someone sabotaged it," I said.

"Sabotage?"

Ava opened her mouth slightly, closed her eyes, and shook her head. "It's a possibility."

"Who would sabotage an underwater electricity plant?" Maya asked.

I didn't reply and didn't need to; my silence was her answer. The saboteur had to be one of them. The islanders had all the reasons in the world to destroy the TOES. To me, they were all suspects. David? Definitely. His bright-toothed father? Sure. Betsy. Derek, despite his disarming tattoos.

Maybe even Maya herself.

5
HAWKING HEADQUARTERS

THE INFLATABLE CRUISED NORTH AWAY FROM *OHANA* and into a cove carved into Nihoa's southern shore. Could my meeting with Maya have gone a little better? Sure. I mean, I kind of accused her and her entire family of sabotage. And she thought I was friends with Steven Hawking, too. That definitely wouldn't score me any points.

Vader sped onto a yellow-white beach. Ashley cut the engine, and it automatically rose up, preventing the propeller blades from crunching into the ground. Hank thought this was wonderful. He even used that very word.

Matt jumped out first, but I was only a second behind. Thankful to be on land again, he crouched and dug his hands into the sand. I did the same, and it felt like baby powder. I was tempted to kick off my high-tops, but Ashley and Steven were already moving, following a narrow path up through the rocks.

We retrieved our backpacks and swung them over our shoulders. In addition to the candy bars, I'd also brought along a few random inventions from Hank's lab. Some of these creations were his own, while others were leftover entries in an annual contest he judged, the Clutterbuck Prize. He was always encouraging us to borrow and test things, so I'd snagged a set of bright yellow shoelaces with a tag that read "SpiderStretch," the high-tops, a pack of gum labeled "Mouthbright," and a few other items. Maybe I'd give Matt the gum if he ran out and his stomach was still queasy. Maybe.

Along with a small telescope, my brother had packed a new camera to photograph the wildlife and a collapsible fishing rod. As for Ava, I don't know what she packed, but she did bring Fred. That's her homemade drone, and as soon as we started walking, she whipped him out of her backpack, powered him up, and tossed him into the air so he could follow us on our trek.

Ashley heard the buzz and turned. "How cute! Steven, where's yours, dear?"

"You know I've grown tired of drones, Ashley," he said. "They're just toys."

On the long, winding trail up the hill we passed green scrubby plants and rock outcroppings spattered with bird droppings. Matt suggested this guano could be a good source of ammonia, a liquid used in the TOES.

"We've already considered that," Steven said. "The problem is that you'd need a way to collect the guano."

"Scraping it off rocks wouldn't work," Ashley added. "You'd need hundreds of people out here working all day."

Hank started laughing. He held his arms out wide. "I'm picturing a whole army of mannequins with removable wide-brimmed hats."

Ava swigged from a water bottle. "Huh?"

For once I was following him. "Because birds love targets, right?"

"Exactly! You could remove the hats every day and harvest the bird poop." He winked my way. The bathroom humor was for me. Hank's way of apologizing for calling me Jake, maybe.

"Speaking of birds," Matt said, pointing to a small, beaked creature hopping across a rock ledge ahead of us. "Is that a Nihoa finch?"

Ashley pretended to pull back on a slingshot. "Bam!" she said. "Those little winged pests are such a migraine."

"But aren't they endangered?" Hank asked.

"Yes, that's the problem!" Ashley said. "If you find any nests on the island, say not a word. Ben and his group have been here a few times, and they're always checking for nests. If they were to find any new ones, they'd have me kicked off Nihoa in a week."

71

"But it would be good news, in terms of the survival of the birds, right?" Matt asked.

"Who cares? They're just birds. We let weak startup companies die off all the time—why not weak species?" She turned and pointed into the distance, where a large, red-footed bird was running toward the edge of a rock, attempting to take off. "Now that beauty, on the other hand . . . that is a creature worth fighting for. Or laughing at. Anyway, onward, up to the house."

While Ashley pressed ahead, the geniuses were paralyzed.

Finally, Matt said, "Was she serious? About the endangered species?"

"I hope not," Hank answered.

Hurrying to catch up to Ashley, we rounded the top of the hill. The path flattened and snaked through low grass and wildflowers before rising again toward the strangest house I'd ever seen. Calling it a home was like calling LeBron James a basketball player. Or Albert Einstein a scientist. Those simple terms just didn't capture the magnificence.

The Hawking house was made entirely from long rectangular steel boxes stacked atop one another. Some were parallel to each other, some perpendicular. Imagine a game of Jenga with blocks the size of school buses. The Hawking home looked like the last few stages of that contest, only the boxes were painted a radiant white. Enormous windows reflected the blue sky and several walls were made entirely of glass.

Ashley stood with her hands on her hips. "It's only temporary, but it's home."

"It's only temporary?"

She made air quotes. "I'm not allowed to build a 'permanent' home here. I'm really only leasing some of the land from the state while we test the TOES. But they did say I could set up a camp, as long as we remove all evidence and imprint when we leave."

"How are you going to remove it?"

"Helicopters, obviously," she said. "We flew it in room by room, and we'll fly it out the same way. But I don't intend to leave anytime soon. We'll be here a few years at least. I've always wanted my own island."

73

"Years?" Steven asked.

He didn't look thrilled, but his mother ignored him. And so did I. "You call this a camp?" I said. I could feel Hank glaring at me. But how was I supposed to remember to be polite and well-mannered in the middle of all this insanity?

"They're all used shipping containers. The helicopters stacked them. One of Kildare's pilot friends did the work. Very skillful. And the whole thing is totally green, too. You can't see from here, but there are solar panels on the roofs, and we harvest rainwater, too. All the floors are bamboo.

We don't use plastic. To be honest, we'll probably have less impact than a regular camp in the end."

"That's amazing," Hank said. "It's so refreshing to meet another person who cares so deeply about the environment."

Ashley laughed. Then she covered her mouth with her hand. "Oh. You were serious? I'm so sorry." She grimaced. "I don't care in the slightest. I just did it this way because it was interesting. Plus it makes me look good."

Once again, Hank was silenced.

Ava hadn't taken her eyes off the building. She piloted Fred to the ground, then packed him away without even looking. "We get to stay there?"

"You do. You each have your own room."

"On the second floor," Steven added. "With views of the ocean."

"In the same hallway as Steven's room," Ashley noted. "So you can all get to know each other."

Ava, Matt, and I didn't need to say a word. We were each getting our own room. And among these rooms, one was probably better than the others. A competition was about to begin. All we needed was a signal. One word from Ashley.

"Go ahead if you like," she said.

She may have continued talking, but once I heard the word go, I was gone. The path was narrow, and Matt was leading, so I had to kind of bounce off a flat boulder to get

74

around him. I'd seen people bust their knees trying that move on reality-TV obstacle courses, but I made it in front of Matt and threw all my energy into that first minute. If I could open a decent lead, then they might give up trying to catch me.

The steep hill nearly killed me, and I reached the doors to Hawking Headquarters sucking in every breath like it was going to be my last. Maybe I should've expected what happened next. I'd spent enough time in Hank's lab and seen enough of his work. I shouldn't have been surprised to step through the steel front doors and see a robot. But I jumped back anyway, startled.

The machine was rolling toward me across the polished bamboo floor. The room itself was about as big as a volleyball court—they must have combined three of those shipping containers to construct it—and several thin white couches were arranged around a coffee table on the far side. As for the robot, it was the size of a small fridge, with two metal arms the size of several linked tennis ball cans and a box-shaped head. Instead of eyes, two camera lenses stared at me, and in the place of a mouth, there was a thin speaker curved in the shape of a smile.

One of its robotic arms held a tray with six sweating glasses. The self-balancing robot rolled forward on two large wheels and spoke with a woman's voice. "Good afternoon, sir. Are you parched?"

"Very," I answered.

The glass was delightfully cold, the lemonade a perfect mix of sour and sweet. I closed my eyes and drank it down in one gulp. Ava and Matt stopped abruptly beside me. "Who's this?" Ava asked.

"I don't know, but she makes delicious lemonade."

Ava circled the robot. "This is an HR-5."

Now Steven caught up. Apparently he'd decided to run along behind us. "You know the model?" he asked.

"Hank has a similar one, an HR-4. We call him Harry. Did you name yours?"

"No, it's a robot," Steven said. "That's ridiculous."

"What about Harriet?"

"Why would I name my robot Harriet?"

I shrugged. "It has a woman's voice."

"What?" Steven stuck out his tongue and sighed dramatically. Then he pulled a smartphone from his back pocket and tapped through a few screens. The robot uttered something in a lifeless, mechanical tone. "There. That's better."

I was still going to call it Harriet.

"You can control it from your phone?" Ava asked.

"Cool," Matt added.

"Yes, well, I can do that and a great deal more. Mine is much more advanced than Hank's model. Ashley got it for me for my twelfth birthday. I've been doing some revolutionary work with it, too. Trying to pass the Turing test," he said, nudging me with his elbow. Then he paused, pursed his lips, and breathed in slowly. "Oh, right," he said, stretching out the words. "You're the other one. You probably don't know."

Before I could respond, a man with shoulder-length brown hair tucked under a straw hat, a thick moustache, and the ugliest Hawaiian shirt I'd ever seen burst through a door near the couches holding a sandwich the size of a football. His shoulders were so narrow that you couldn't tell where his neck ended and his arms began. Yet his hips were almost as wide as a hula hoop. With his free hand he pushed the hat back on his head and studied us with surprise. A small garden's worth of lettuce was sticking out the sides of his sandwich, along with the corners of several orange-colored slices of cheese. Smells of cheddar and ham were forcing their way through a cloud of cologne.

"Steven!" the man boomed. "The birthday boy!"

"Oh," Steven said. "You're here."

A girl popped out behind him, holding a phone just below her chin. She looked to be a little younger than Ava and me—I'd guess eleven or so. Fifth grade, most likely. Her hair was pulled back in a mess of a ponytail. There was a dollop of ketchup near the left side of her mouth. Someone needed to give her a napkin. She waved to Ava. My sister smiled back, and the girl quickly stared down at her phone.

Behind them, the door swung in and out before settling to a stop. Now I smelled chicken fingers. Were they trying to tease us? I was suddenly starving.

"Hi, Mr. Hawking," the girl said, looking up again.

"Greetings, Clementine," Steven said. "I must be going. It's time for my lab hours."

"You have a lab in here?" Ava asked.

"Of course," Steven snapped. "I'd invite you to have a look, but I wouldn't want you stealing any of my ideas. Until later, then?"

Matt followed Steven upstairs, insisting that he had to study for his test. "Don't pick a room without us," I called out to him.

"They're all identical," the man said. "Believe me, you'll be pleased. My daughter and I are here for the birthday party. You?"

"Sort of," Ava said.

"They're very good friends, my Clementine and Steven."

The girl stayed focused on her phone as she answered, "Not really. I barely know him. And he makes me call him Mr. Hawking."

"Don't be silly, dear," he said, patting her head. Then he noticed his mustard-smeared palm, checked her hair, and made a small O with his mouth. A yellow streak was now crossing the part in her hair. He shoved one end of the sandwich into his mouth and gnawed off an impressive section. After only a few chews, he asked, "What are your names?"

"I'm Jack," I said, extending my hand. Quickly I pulled it back and waved instead. "A friend of Steven's, I guess. That was Matt. This is Ava. We're visiting from New York."

Before the man could reply, the robot rolled between us. Surprised, Ava moved away, then circled the machine, studying its head and muttering something about microphones.

"New York! I had no idea he had friends in New York. That must be four friends now. Even five? Who's keeping count, though, right?"

I waited, thinking the man was going to introduce himself. But he just kept on chewing. His daughter, Clementine, remained at his side, but she was in another world—an electronic one. I tried to see what she was doing on her phone. An app? A game? I couldn't tell. "What's your name, sir?" I asked at last.

The man chomped deeper into his sandwich, then laughed through the lettuce and shook his head. "Of course! New York. How could you know me? I mean, everyone in the islands knows me. This is my daughter, Clementine, and I am Albert Charles Krumplitch, but they call me the A.C. king, or just the king."

I nodded. "Oh. Why?"

79

"My initials! A.C.K.—air-conditioning king? I've got the biggest air-conditioning business in the islands. I keep Hawaii cool, my friend. Without me, I don't even think people would live here. That's the truth."

The front doors opened behind us. "Albert. Clementine. You're here." Ashley stood with Hank at her side. Her smile was about as fake as a plastic flower. "Glad to see you helped yourself to some provisions."

The king strode past me with his arms spread wide. A huge piece of cheese dropped out of the sandwich and onto the floor. Ashley turned her head to the side as he moved in to hug her. That was my cue. Ava was still in robot world, so I tipped the lid of an imaginary hat at Hank, nodded to Clementine, who was still centered entirely on her phone, and hurried up the stairs.

A young woman with wild curly hair and thin rectangular glasses was hurrying down. I waved and said hello. She smiled awkwardly and said nothing.

If nothing else, I decided, this place was going to be interesting.

Three linked shipping containers formed the upstairs hallway. There were six doors on the right side and, I guessed, six additional steel boxes branching off at right angles. Each one a bedroom. I tried the first door, but it was locked. "Not this one," Steven called out from inside. So that was his lab. I

80

tried the next door. Locked as well. "Or that one!" he yelled. "That's my room."

The next door was open slightly. My brother was inside, on the bed, staring at numbers on his screen. The fourth room would be mine, and it was magnificent. A massive bed, a desk, and a sitting area with a couch and a coffee table. All to myself. Even the art was cool. Prints of Chinese characters hung on the walls to my right and left. And I wouldn't have to look up that Sun guy after all. A copy of his book, *The Art of War*, was waiting on my bedside table.

The far wall was one huge floor-to-ceiling window overlooking the Pacific Ocean. The edge of the cliff was almost directly below. I was afraid to get too close, so I remained a few steps back and just stared.

Blue. Everything was blue. The scene was so full of water and sky that I began to wonder if there even was a world out there beyond the horizon. What if we'd been transported to some extra dimension? One where they really did have planes made out of underwear and electric-eel-powered cars? When we followed Hank around, anything seemed possible.

The view wasn't the only surprise. Each of us also had a wide, thin, crystal-clear television. On the nightstand next to my enormous bed lay a brand-new phone. I swiped the screen. No password. At least a hundred apps. A strong Wi-Fi signal, and a screen so high-definition I felt like I could reach right into it and pluck a flower from the background image. I assumed someone had left it there, but then a message popped up on the screen. I read it and ran next door to Matt's room. "These are ours?" I asked.

He actually looked away from his work. "Cool, right?"

Yes, that was one word. Or you could call it amazing. Fantastic. Outrageous. Any of those would've worked, too. I was starting to think that I liked Ashley Hawking. Maybe I could even be friends with Steven. Did that make me a bad person? Actually, don't answer that.

At lunch, I wolfed down a sandwich huge enough to feed a bear. Cold cuts alone were not enough. When no one was looking, I jammed a few warm chicken nuggets in there as well. Hank wasn't comfortable with my appetite, though. He actually wanted to call Min to see if eating something that large was safe for a twelve-year-old. That's what he claimed, anyway. But Ava said he just wanted an excuse to chat. She's convinced they're secretly dating.

Afterward, Matt hurried back to his room to study while the rest of us toured the so-called camp with Ashley, Steven, and Kildare. The house was more crowded that I would've expected. At least a dozen people were rushing around cleaning, working in the kitchen, and offering us drinks and snacks on silver trays. The king and Clementine were staying on the first floor; that's where Ashley's room was as well. We weren't allowed to visit Steven's room or his lab—Ashley confessed that he didn't even let her inside. But the bazillionaire's office was an interesting spot, filled with a wall of monitors but no chairs. She said she preferred to remain on her feet. Otherwise, the house had two kitchens, two dining rooms, and an exercise space. Ashley proudly noted that there were whiteboard walls all over—you could draw up or write out your ideas just about anywhere you wanted. Hank actually clapped when he heard that.

On the roof, Ashley had set up a small observatory with three telescopes. Hank forced Matt to join us for that part, and my brother was practically skipping on our way back down.

That night, the whole group of us gathered for dinner, including Rosa, who'd finished her work in the lab for the day, and Kildare. The chef, a bald, tattooed man with a sprig of parsley sticking out of the corner of his mouth, explained the meal before serving us, and it was so delicious I barely spoke. I devoured two of the juiciest steaks in history and a full head of broccoli. And I don't even like broccoli. I would've eaten this weird potato thing he'd made, too, but the king was sitting across from me, shoveling mounds of the buttery mush into his mouth. Seeing the little clumps of potato clinging to his moustache crushed my appetite. For a little while, anyway. Then dessert arrived.

We were digging into mountains of pineapple sorbet doused with hot fudge when Ashley outlined the submarine trip she wanted to take with Hank. "It's simple, really," she insisted. "We dive down, inspect the pipe to see if something's broken or busted, maybe take a few pictures, then ride back up."

"In a submarine?" the king asked. "That sounds about as simple as installing central air in a cave." He leaned toward me over the table. In a low voice, he added, "That's very difficult to do, if you're wondering. But I've done it."

To be polite I nodded.

"I don't know," Hank said. He started moving his jaw from side to side.

"Can you do it remotely?" Ava asked.

"The *Nautilus* isn't set up for that," Hank noted.

"Diving that deep is not that big of a deal," Steven claimed. "I've been down to fifteen hundred feet in a submarine off Kauai."

"You have?" Hank asked.

"Six months ago," Ashley said, "with a guide on Kauai who runs tours in his two-person submarine. Incidentally, I checked with him, too, but he's been totally unresponsive. You'd be surprised how difficult it is to get a deep-sea submarine on short notice. So what do you think? Tomorrow morning?"

"But we just got here."

"Why wait?" Ashley asked. "I despise waiting. I don't think I've stood in a line since I was in high school."

Hank pinched his nose with his fingers. His cheeks puffed. His eyes reddened, and he dropped his hands to the table as if he was trying to steady himself. "No," he said. "I can't do it." He tapped his ears with his index fingers. "Sinus infection of some sort. Lingering cold from our trip down to the South Pole, I suppose. I'm not fit to dive. Can't we wait a few days?"

"No," Ashley insisted.

"The weather may turn," Kildare explained, "but tomorrow is going to be clean and clear."

Ashley pushed away her dish of sorbet, stared down at the table, and leaned back in her chair. "I guess I could go alone."

Something about her suggestion bothered me. I couldn't place it, exactly. The way she avoided eye contact. The tone of her voice. That move to push her dessert away. I had this strange feeling that she was acting, and that she really did want to go down there all alone. But why? Why would she want to inspect the bottom of the pipe without anyone?

Steven pointed at Matt and Ava with his sorbet spoon.

"Why don't you send one of them instead?" he asked. "You shouldn't have to go, Ashley."

"I'd like to, Steven."

Ava motioned to the prince. "Why don't you go with her?"

"Been there, done that," Steven replied. "The sea no longer interests me."

Matt glanced at Hank, then offered, "I'll go with you, Ashley."

I glared across the table at my suddenly adventurous brother. He couldn't even stomach a ride in the underplane. Now he was volunteering to dive down to the seafloor in a homemade submarine? Ashley leaned back in her chair and studied Matt for a moment. "No," she concluded. "Not with your weak stomach. Kildare, you're too stressful." Then she pointed to the king, who was stealing sorbet from his unnaturally quiet daughter. "Obviously you won't fit." Finally, she addressed Rosa. "And you, my dear, are far too tall."

"That's fine with me," Rosa responded. "I prefer a nice, dry lab."

Would Ava volunteer? I didn't think so. But I wasn't sure I knew what my siblings were going to do anymore. So I couldn't risk it. In our group, I was the adventurer. I was the one who took chances. So I raised my hand.

"Another question, Jack?" Steven sneered.

"No, I'm volunteering. I'm game."

"You?" Ashley asked. Her voice rose at the end; she was genuinely surprised.

"No, Jack, absolutely not," Hank said.

He didn't protest when Matt volunteered. Why me? Now I almost did want to go. Just to show him that I could. "Why not?" I asked. "What's wrong with me?"

"Your tie, for one," Steven said.

That hurt. My bow tie had little cartoon fish hooks, and the blue background matched my socks. "Why can't I go?" I asked.

"Because the pressure at that depth would be more than nine hundred pounds per square inch!" Hank said, his voice rising in pitch with each word. "That nicely shaped head of yours could very well implode."

87

Rosa leaned forward and looked down the table at Hank. "But he would be safely inside the *Nautilus Redux*."

"Which hasn't been tested at those kinds of depths," Ava noted.

"Min wouldn't approve," Hank muttered. "She'd kill me."

"Min's not here, and it wouldn't be her choice, anyway," Matt replied. Normally he'd never argue with Hank like that, but my brother hated any suggestion that someone else was in charge of us. Sure, we were still kids. Physically, at least. But in the legal sense, we were adults. We'd been living on our own for more than a year.

I watched Ashley. She scratched her bright red hair and ran her thumbs across her thin eyebrows.

"Jack will be fine," Matt said.

Silently, I appealed to Ava for help. She held up her hands. She wasn't getting involved. This was my call.

"I inspected the sub earlier," Rosa added. "It's remarkably well built, Hank. I wouldn't worry, Jack."

"Seriously! Have some confidence in your design, Hank!" Ashley said. She lifted her glass in my direction. "I'll look out for Jack. At the very slightest indication of danger, we'll pop right back up." She traced a cross on her chest. "Promise."

Hank wouldn't look at her. Or me. He breathed in through his teeth, then said, "I don't . . ."

88

"He does look a little frightened," Steven said. "Maybe you should sleep on it, Jack?"

And that decided everything for me. One little remark from Steven, along with a question as subtle as a samurai's sword. "No," I said. "I'm going. I trust you, Hank." And then, although I didn't mean it, I added, "And you, Ashley."

Hank threw his hands in the air, accidentally sending his spoon across the room, where it bounced off a sculpture of a mermaid. Then he yelled, "Fine! Go! I can't stop you."

No, maybe not. But soon I was wishing he had.

6

A DANGEROUS DECISION

LATER, IN MY ROOM, WITH THE DARK OCEAN SPREADING out under the dark sky, I wondered what I'd done. Was this really a victory? I was always trying to work myself up to genius status, or at the very least the rank of nerd. But smart people don't jump off bridges on dares. They don't allow themselves to be talked into terribly dangerous situations by mean-spirited brats. And they definitely don't climb into untested submarines just to prove they're brave. I sat up in bed, flicked on the beautiful flat-screen, then turned it off again about five seconds later. I read the first chapter of *The Art of War* about seventeen times, but I didn't even yawn.

At one point, while staring up at the ceiling, I started wondering. What if there was another way out of this situation? Maybe I could sneak away, hide on the other side of the island for a few days, and claim I was kidnapped by natives.

No. That wouldn't hold. The natives were dentists.

Faking an injury was a possibility. Or a sinus infection? I stood up and walked to the window. Steven would call me out if I tried to claim I wasn't fit to ride. I had to go. And I'd probably be fine. Ashley wouldn't risk her own life just to explore a pipe. Or at least I didn't think so.

Ava opened my door and leaned in. "You know there's Netflix on the television, right?"

I didn't. That would help. A few episodes of *Duck Detective* would certainly take my mind off things. "Where's Matt?"

"Studying again," she said. "But he said he might take a break to test his new telescope in a little bit if you want to join us on the roof."

"No, I'm good. I'm going to do a little more reading."

"Really?"

"Yes."

Well, sort of, anyway. During dinner, before we started talking about the morning's mission, I filled up an entire page of my notebook with terms I didn't understand. Most of them related to the undersea world beneath the lab—the strange life-forms that lurked in the dark waters. Now that I was scheduled to descend with Ashley, I really needed to know more about that world.

Matt leaned into the doorway next to Ava. They

exchanged a look, then Ava spoke. "Are you sure you want to do this tomorrow?"

I shrugged. "It'll be fine."

"You don't have to go," Matt said. "Ashley could just pilot the sub herself."

I motioned for them to step inside and close the door.

"I was thinking that, too, at first," I said. "But then it seemed like she almost wanted to go alone."

"So?"

"So what if it's her? What if she's the one sabotaging the power plant?"

"That doesn't make any sense," Ava said.

Matt was quiet. That was encouraging. "What did we learn down at the South Pole?" I asked.

"We learned about extreme creatures, melting ice shelves, sea ice," Matt said.

"I learned a lot about engineering machines to survive in extreme conditions."

For geniuses, they could really be clueless sometimes. "No! You're missing the point. We learned that everyone is a suspect. Everyone!" The third episode of *Duck Detective*, in which the heroic sleuth has to interrogate an entire barn full of creatures, drove home the same lesson. But I kept that to myself. I didn't want my siblings to know I was teaching myself about detective work by watching a show about a fowl.

"Everyone?" Matt pressed.

"Everyone," I repeated. "Even Ashley."

"He accused Maya and the islanders, too," Ava noted.

"Slick," Matt said.

Ava walked to the window, stared down at the water, then stepped back. "Why would she sabotage her own project?"

"I don't know," I admitted. "But a little time in that steel bubble tomorrow might help me figure that out."

We stared at each other in silence.

"I think you're crazy," Ava said.

"I wish I could go instead," Matt added. "You're going to see some amazing things. Oh, and I think you're crazy, too."

"Thank you. That means a lot."

After two hours of reading, I tried to sleep, but the moonlight was shining in like a gray spotlight. At one point I lay perfectly still for what felt like two days, terrified that the slightest movement on my part would topple our Jenga tower and send us all tumbling down the hillside into the sea. I downloaded about twenty games on the new phone and played each one for about a minute.

When Hank woke me the next morning, I felt like I'd been asleep for all of two minutes. "You ready?" he asked.

"Give me a few minutes. I'll meet you downstairs."

During the night I'd laid out some clothes on a chair,

but my outfit seemed a little formal for a submarine dive, even if the bow tie did feature little octopi. So I threw on a T-shirt, shorts, and sandals. Then I filled my backpack with a sweatshirt, a pair of socks in case it got cold, and a few of the items from Hank's lab. My new phone was already dead, so I plugged it in, then checked to make sure I had the gum; chewing helped pop my ears on airplanes. Maybe it would work in a submarine, too.

Downstairs, Matt, Ava, and Hank were sitting on the couches talking to Ashley. She pointed to a tray on the coffee table with several glasses of freshly squeezed juice.

"Try some," Matt suggested, holding out a glass of the reddish-brown drink. His tone sounded genuine, but in his eyes I could see a serious warning. He was silently telling me not to let that stuff anywhere near my taste buds.

"Do you have coffee?" I asked.

"You drink coffee?"

"I drink coffee."

A little, anyway. A small cup now and then. In the past, when grown-ups would look at me funny after learning of my love for brewed beans, I'd point out that a hundred years ago, kids my age drank coffee all the time. But then Matt noted that they also worked full-time jobs and only lived until they were about fifty, if they were lucky. So I trashed that argument.

Ashley pointed to the open door behind her. "The coffee should be on the counter in the eat-in kitchen," she said. "Ring the bell if you need anything. One of my Oompa-Loompas in the main kitchen will hear you."

At that point, I was ready to believe anything, but I should've known better than to ask my next question. "Wait, you have Oompa-Loompas here?"

"No, that's just what I call my staff." She leaned over to Hank and added, "They love it."

I doubted that, and I decided that I'd find the coffee on my own, without bothering one of them. Through the door, the eat-in kitchen was ridiculously clean and so bright that I had to squint. A square island with a marble countertop occupied the center of the rectangular room. Tall stools were arranged around the outside, and there was a small sink at one end. Kildare leaned against the counter on the opposite side, drinking coffee with his back to me, reading on an iPad. I coughed. Immediately he folded the soft case over the screen of his tablet.

The detective in me was immediately curious. What had he been reading? And why was he suddenly smiling at me? "Good morning," I said.

His eyes were dark and small. The skin around them was too wrinkled and creased for someone his age, and his stare was like some kind of laser beam. I wanted to duck or bob around to avoid it, like a boxer trying to dodge a jab. But the coffeepot on the island called to me first. I poured a small cup.

"I was drinking six mugs a day at your age," he said.

Did that explain the wrinkled eyes? Maybe I'd have to cut down my intake. "One is fine for me."

"Where's your phone?" he asked.

"My phone?"

"The one you got last night."

"In my room, charging," I said. "Why?"

"You should keep it charged. And carry it with you."

"Why?"

He avoided my question. "You're the one going down in the tin can, right?" I nodded over the rim of my coffee cup. He removed a small locket on a chain from his pocket and tossed it to me. "Wear this. It's good luck."

The tarnished metal locket had a hinge and a small clip. I opened it, revealing a portrait of a cat. Was he serious? Apparently so: I looked up and didn't see even a flicker of a smile. "Thank you," I said.

"That's Mr. Winkles," Kildare responded. "I brought him with me on every dive I ever did as a SEAL."

The actual cat? Or the picture? I wasn't sure, but something about Kildare told me not to ask. Mr. Winkles had a menacing look to him. Or maybe that was just me. There's something about cats that terrifies me. The way they stalk around and look you right in the eyes—I don't know; I guess I feel like if the world comes to an end, and humanity is extinguished like a snuffed candle, I could see the cats being behind it all. But I would've thrown a hundred cat necklaces over my head if there was a chance they were going to keep me safe. "I'll keep him close," I said.

Although it was only partially charged, I grabbed my phone from the room. After a trip in *Vader* out to the lab, Ashley and I were soon climbing into the *Nautilus Redux*. Kildare, Rosa, Hank, and my siblings were all there to see us descend, but Steven couldn't join us. Lab hours, he claimed. Hank made me put on the socks I'd packed, insisting that it would be cold at depth. And yes, they looked ridiculous with the sandals.

The submarine was named after the starring vehicle in Jules Verne's *Twenty Thousand Leagues Under the Sea*, a book that had already helped me once, down at the South Pole. In the novel, though, the *Nautilus* is pretty much an underwater yacht. Hank's version was about the size of one of those miniature Smart cars. A thick cable extended from the top of the submarine to an enormous winch on the deck of the moon pool. The cable would remain attached throughout our dive, sending a live video feed to everyone in the lab.

The *Nautilus* was shaped like a giant bubble, with four

propellers at the back and two headlights the size of basket-balls out front, right below a large, round window. Hank was saying something about how he'd used parts of old cars to build the frame, but I pretended I didn't hear that. I leaned over the water to peek inside. My phone slid out of my shirt pocket, bounced off the side of the submarine, and dropped into the water with a heartbreaking plunk.

"So that happened," Ava said.

My soul was shattered. My new phone, gone. Soon to be snapped up by some teenage mermaid desperate to snap undersea selfies. I glanced up at Ashley. Would she give me another one? I was dealing with a bazillionaire, after all.

She was halfway into the submarine. "I'm not giving you another one," she said. "Are you two being careful with yours?"

"I had them leave their phones in their rooms," Hank said.

"Try to keep them on you from now on," Kildare cut in. "For emergencies."

"Sorry," Hank said, "it's just that I despise those devices. All these texting tweens are going to end up with long-term thumb and neck injuries. Not to mention that the phone must remove at least twenty IQ points from the developing brain. Granted, I don't believe in the IQ test, exactly. But I do find it's a decent measure of potential."

In a whisper so loud it was nearly a shout, Ashley added, "Steven scored nearly one hundred and sixty."

Ava smirked. Her score was higher.

I climbed in through the hatch and sat beside Ashley. There was some room for my backpack behind me, but that was all. Matt definitely would not have been able to jam his long legs inside. I couldn't see how Hank even fit. And the small size wasn't the only problem. The submarine was all about science, not comfort, so the seats were about as cushy as folding chairs. And no one told me what I was supposed to do if I had to go to the bathroom. As Matt, Ava, and Rosa watched from the tiled deck, Hank leaned in through the hatch, reached down, and tightened my harness. I patted the Mr. Winkles locket hanging around my neck. "How long is this trip again?" I asked.

"Are you sure you want to go?" Hank whispered.

Of course not! But I wasn't going to admit that now. "I'm ready."

"Good!" Ashley said.

"Really?" Hank asked.

I couldn't look at Ava or Matt, so I focused on the control panel in front of me, which resembled something out of an old movie—all plastic buttons and switches and gauges. "Really, I'm ready."

"Okay, then. Good luck!"

And Hank closed the hatch.

A few more questions and I might have caved. One, even. One more question about whether I really wanted to dive two thousand feet—or two Eiffel Towers stacked on top of each other, as Ava put it—in a tiny submersible and I would've jumped out and run. Or maybe I would've wriggled my jaw a little, wondering aloud whether I, too, had a sinus infection. Then I would've insisted on braving the journey anyway, but they would've forced me out to preserve my health. That way, I would've earned their respect because I'd begged to go down, but I wouldn't have had to risk my life. Really, that would've been perfect.

But that's not how it happened.

Ashley flipped several rows of switches. Her long, ringed fingers danced across a series of bright-red plastic buttons on the control panel. "No touchscreen?" I asked.

"That's what I love about the design," she said. "It's all analog. Old-school, and far more reliable at these depths."

This was the moment she was supposed to ask me if I was ready to dive. But she skipped that step, and we sank into the deep blue water.

7

TWO THOUSAND FEET DOWN

MAYBE I'VE SAID THIS BEFORE, BUT ONE OF THE ways to keep pace with the geniuses is to outread them. And I'm not talking about novels or comic books, unfortunately. I mean the kind of reading that stuffs your brain with facts. On our way to the South Pole I read nearly five books about the place in three days. And the night before I climbed into the *Nautilus Redux*, I'd tried to learn as much as I possibly could about two different subjects. The first was this weird power plant Rosa Morris had built. The other was the area of the ocean we were going to explore. One fancy name for it was the mesopelagic zone. Some called it the disphotic zone. But I preferred the third version: the twilight zone.

Unfortunately, there was some waiting to do before we reached that depth. And not much else. Look, I'm not going to say I was bored as we dropped. That would be crazy. Totally. And Hank doesn't like us using the word bored anyway. He says that if someone is bored, it's because the person is boring. But to be perfectly honest, the view wasn't all that exciting for the first twenty minutes. The water was crowded with plankton and krill and other tiny little creatures. The blue slowly turned darker and darker, as if black dye were seeping up from below. But otherwise it was all kind of the same, until Ashley spotted my phone drifting slowly down. The water glowed below it; apparently the screen was still working. I pressed my fingers to the cold, damp Plexiglass. My first true love, lost forever.

A few minutes later, I asked Ashley if I could borrow her phone, mostly out of boredom. I was shocked to see she had a game called Chicken Racer, which is kind of like Street Racer, only you ride on the back of a chicken. After ten terribly short minutes, Ashley took her phone back. But the battery was nearly dead anyway, and the world around us was getting more interesting.

A round speaker on the control panel buzzed. "You're entering the disphotic zone now," Hank said.

"Did you get a good score, Jack?" Matt asked.

I jumped a little at the sound of their voices. I'd forgotten that Hank, Ava, and Matt could see and hear everything because of the cable, which was basically a giant extension cord that transmitted power, video, and communications. Cameras inside and outside the submarine captured all the sounds and views and sent them up to the lab. I guess this was good, since I didn't feel like I was completely stuck in there on my own with Ashley. But then she released a unique bodily breeze, and I wished they could smell what was happening, too. I don't know if it was the result of that strange juice on the coffee table, but the air was poisoned, and I wanted Matt to catch a whiff. I pinched my nose and pulled my shirt up over my mouth.

"*Photic* is a version of *photos*, the Greek word for 'light,'" Ava added.

I did not say "I know," but I honestly did. All that reading the night before was pretty useful. Ashley, Matt, and Hank started knocking facts at us like we were the targets on a firing range, but I'll spare you the know-it-all chatter and inform you myself. The big thing to remember about the twilight zone is that no sunlight reaches down here. And since there's no sunlight, there's no photosynthesis—the process plants use to convert the sun's rays into energy. Basically, we eat food for energy, but plants eat light. Kind of like Superman, who gets his powers from the sun.

Anyway, underwater plants like sea grass and kelp use photosynthesis, since sunlight leaks down through the water. But when you drop below about six hundred feet, the light from the sun can't tunnel down that far. Those kinds of plants just don't exist. But the creatures down there have to eat something. So what do they snack on? Well, each other, naturally. But they also feed on something called marine snow.

This isn't like normal snow. Instead of pure white frozen crystals, the marine version is made up of all the dead plants and fish and plankton that drop down from the light-drenched water above. That's part of it, anyway. The rest of these little underwater snowflakes trickle down from the undersides of all those swimming creatures above. Basically, marine snow is part fish poop. And we were soaring through a blizzard of the stuff.

Ashley switched on the headlights. For ten or twenty feet in front of us the water glowed blue, but beyond that it was all darkness. She turned the submarine, and we could just make out the pipe. "That's part of the TOES, right?"

"Correct," she said. "We're following that all the way down. But I don't want to get too close."

I coughed. The air inside was dry and cold, and it still stank of a terrible mixture of bazillionaire farts and her manly underarm deodorant.

"Are you sick?" Ashley asked.

I was wondering the same thing about her.

"What are you seeing?" Matt asked. He sounded both jealous and excited.

"The picture we're getting from the sub's exterior cameras

isn't all that great," Hank explained. "The video is kind of dark."

"I'm not seeing much," I answered. Then I realized that I was missing a fantastic opportunity. "Wait . . . I do see something. What is that? Ashley, are you . . . it's coming closer! Noooooooo!!!!!"

Ashley sighed.

"It's not that bad, Jack," Matt said.

"Don't forget there are cameras inside, too," Ava added.

Right. I waved at the tiny lens above us.

They could see us clearly, but they couldn't smell inside. And the bazillionaire had struck again. I would've cut off my nose if that had been an option.

"Really, tell us, Jack," Hank said. "Are you experiencing anything unusual?"

"It's getting colder."

"And darker," Ashley said.

I coughed again. "Dry in here, too."

Ava started thinking aloud. "Maybe it needs some kind of humidity system, Hank."

"Unfortunately, that dryness is part of the air circulation system," he explained.

"Whoa! Are those bristlemouths?" Matt asked.

I leaned forward. Hundreds of fish, each one about the size of my hand, were clustering near the light, following us as we dropped. They had large eyes, small tail fins, and jaws that looked big enough for a creature ten times their size. A bell rang in my head. I knew these little guys. I'd read about them.

Ashley gazed at them, her mouth hanging open in wonder. She clasped her hands behind her head. "These creatures are more numerous than people," she said.

"And we didn't even know they existed until William Beebe dropped down in his bathysphere," Hank added, his voice chopped by static. "The deep ocean is the next great frontier for exploration. There's a whole other world down there that we know almost nothing about."

The swarm of fish gathering around our lights thickened.

"Are you seeing this?" Ashley asked.

"Light is an enormous draw in the disphotic zone," Hank explained. "Lantern fish generate a light to draw in curious prey, then gobble them up."

We kept dropping. At times, the pipe would come into view, but Ashley was careful to keep a safe distance. The air kept getting colder and drier. Every few minutes Hank would ask us how the *Nautilus* was holding up, and when Ashley would reply that nothing was leaking, he almost sounded surprised.

Finally, we approached the base of the pipe.

"You should be about twenty feet away now," Hank said.

"We're losing a little clarity. Is there something blocking the camera?"

"Jack, did you press the wrong button or something?"

"No, I didn't even—"

The submarine jerked and spun forward. My backpack fell onto the control panel. Suddenly we were heading straight down toward the seafloor. If not for the harness, I would've slammed into the windshield. The speaker blasted out static, then clicked off. The green light above the communications panel blinked, flickered, and darkened. Silence. The lights inside the cabin dimmed. Ashley was frantically working the controls. Finally the submarine spun again, and we were sitting upright.

"What was that?" I asked.

She toggled a few switches back and forth, then sat back and crossed her forearms on her stomach. "Hmm," she said.

Hmm? We were trapped in a little homemade submarine in utter darkness, hovering below two thousand feet of water, and that was all she could say? I needed more. "Are we okay?" I asked.

"We seem to have lost contact with the surface." Yeah. Got that. "And the lights dimmed." Noticed that, too. "So I have to wonder if we somehow broke loose of the cable, in which case we're running on batteries now."

107

Which meant what? I gave her a second to explain. She did not. "So," I said again, "are we going to be okay?"

Ashley smiled and shrugged. "I believe so. Right? Yes, definitely. We should be fine. But let's start heading up just in case."

This was probably the right idea. The safe plan. But we were here. I stared out in the direction of the pipe. The water was murky. We'd have to steer in closer to see anything. But we weren't coming back down anytime soon. Not if the *Nautilus Redux* was damaged. If we ascended, this whole trip would be a waste. Was this part of her plan? Was this the game all along? Maybe she wanted this mission to fail. I should've been watching her, but the sea outside was too distracting. I'd been acting like some kind of scientific tourist, not a seasoned duck detective. Or a human one. If she had flipped some switch shutting off the communications, or even disconnecting us from the cable, I wouldn't have noticed. So now I had to test her.

"Wait," I said. "We're only twenty feet away, right?"

"Roughly."

"Shouldn't we cruise in a little closer for a quick peek?"

"No. We should go up."

"Would it really be riskier to go ten feet closer?"

Ashley squinted at the control panel. She hummed an unfamiliar tune. I braced, ready for her to yell or threaten me or wonder aloud how in the world I had unraveled her carefully crafted plot—how an otherwise average young man with a fondness for bow ties had outsmarted a bazillionaire computer scientist.

I was ready for all that and more.

But then she surprised me.

"You're right, Jack. Let's keep going."

"Excuse me?"

"We're here. We might as well scoot in a little closer."

If she was guilty, why was she giving in so easily? This wasn't the decision of a woman who was trying to thwart an investigation. Her decision wrecked my entire theory. And it was also about as smart as an old shoe. "I changed my mind," I said. "Let's go up."

She ignored me, steering the craft closer. "The base of the pipe should be about ten feet away now," she said.

The scene was as dark as a basement corner. "I can't even see anything," I said. "The headlights aren't working."

"We just need to get closer," she said. "Since we're only on battery power, all the electricity is going to the interior systems, not the headlights. But that's an interesting idea, Jack."

I had an idea? "Wait, what?"

She started humming again before explaining. "Yes, definitely. If I turn off the interior lights and the heater, the

109

headlights might start working again. It will be cold in here. And dark. But we should be able to get a much clearer view of the base."

"And then we can switch everything back?"

"In theory."

Part of me wanted to beg her to get us back to the surface as soon as possible, but this was our chance. We couldn't give up now. "Let's try it," I said, my voice shaky.

My backpack had fallen onto my lap, and while Ashley flipped a few switches, I reached inside, found the pack of gum, removed a piece, and started chewing. Before the mildly minty flavor began to spread, the cabin dropped into darkness.

The headlights switched on, illuminating the scene.

The world outside glowed an eerie blue.

The base of the pipe was only a body length away, and our questions were answered immediately. I'm no Ava. I'm not fluent in the language of machines. But even I could tell that something was drastically wrong. The steel base was jagged, and a huge, circular metal screen hung off the bottom. "That doesn't look good," I said.

"No, no it doesn't. What could have done that?"

She wasn't asking me, really. She was thinking aloud. But I had to stop myself from replying. *Don't say eels*, I told myself. *Don't say eels.*

"It looks like some kind of explosive," she said. Then she shook her head and, with the heel of her hand, pressed the same button on the control panel ten times in a row, with a few seconds' break between each jab. Taking pictures with the camera, I guessed. "I think we've seen enough," she decided.

She flicked off the headlights. The darkness swallowed us. I waited for the cabin lights and the heat to come back on. And waited. I heard her flipping switches, rapidly clicking. But nothing was happening. I really wanted to hear Hank's voice again. Even an insulting comment from Matt would've been welcome. "Ashley? What's going on?"

"The lights, the heat—they've shut down. There's a button to reboot the battery power, but . . ."

"But what?"

She exhaled. "But I forget where it is, and I can't even see the control panel."

"Can't we just go up now?"

"No. If I can't reboot the batteries, I can't empty the ballast tanks."

And if she couldn't pump the water out of the ballast tanks, they wouldn't fill with air. And if they didn't fill with air, we wouldn't be able to float back to the surface.

So, yeah.

This was a problem.

111

"Where's my phone?" she demanded.

I felt around and found it on the dashboard. "I don't think you'll get a signal." She grabbed it, then growled in frustration as the phone made a strange, almost sad noise. "What? What's wrong?"

"It's dead," she said. "And I didn't want to call anyone. I was going to use it as a flashlight. But now I'm out of power because you were playing that stupid chicken racing game."

I opened my mouth to reply. But everything she'd said was true. Except, maybe, for the part about the game being stupid. Besides, if it was so bad, why did she have it on her phone?

Nervous, I started chewing faster.

Ashley's face began to glow.

"What's that?" she asked. "Where's that light coming from?"

The light faded. "What light?"

"What were you doing? Did you touch something?"

"No!"

"Your mouth . . . it's coming from your mouth." The light glowed again. The gum! I'd grabbed it off the table in Hank's lab, along with the high-tops. What was it called? Mouthbright. I hadn't thought about it when I threw it in my pack. And I didn't really see why anyone would invent gum that glowed when you chewed it. But I didn't care. At that moment, down in that dark submarine, Mouthbright was right up there with the nose vacuum as one of the greatest inventions in human history. "Keep chewing!" she said. "With your mouth open, so the light can shine."

The harder I chewed and the more my lips smacked, the brighter the light glowed.

"Over here," she said, grabbing me by the shirt and pulling me closer to the control panel. "If Steven were here he could have worked this out in the dark. He has a photographic memory." A bad taste spread through my mouth; it reminded me of a spoiled lemon. Was I becoming allergic to Steven Hawking? Or was the gum turning? "Ah, there!" she exclaimed. She slammed down a button with the heel of her right hand.

Instantly, the lights glowed. The heater hummed. Ashley flipped another switch, and the sound that followed reminded me of both an emptying bathtub and a powerfully whirring fan. "What is that?" I asked.

"The ballast tanks are pumping out water and filling with compressed air from a pair of SCUBA tanks."

"So we're going up?"

"We're going up, Jack," she said, "and we are going to figure out what in the world happened down here."

113

8

AN AQUATIC
INVESTIGATION

YOU'D THINK I'D GET SOME SERIOUS SYMPATHY AFTER an experience like that. A little praise, maybe. A few nice words about my bravery. Some congratulations for the way I remained so calm in such a tense situation. But no. After a long, slow ascent, Ashley and I climbed out of the submarine onto the tiled deck, and all I got were a few quick embraces, a one-armed guy hug from Matt, who for some reason was soaking wet, and a firm pat on the back from Kildare, who then pointed to the Mr. Winkles charm under my shirt. All that was over in about twenty seconds. I barely even got any credit for the Mouthbright gum. Hank cringed when I mentioned it—he said he despised the gum because it encouraged people to chew with their mouths open.

Mostly, everyone just wanted to talk about the submarine, the busted pipe, and what they'd been through, too. Ava explained that the power had gone out in the lab at the same time the cable snapped free of the submarine. Apparently no one had ever let the cable out that far. The end wasn't well connected to the big steel spool on the deck of the moon pool, so it just popped loose, and we were left dangling down there like a steel yo-yo freed from a two-thousand-foot-long string. Then it took them ten minutes to activate the backup power system in the lab and, in the confusion, Matt had fallen into the pool. Unfortunately, no one had thought to film the moment. I scanned the room. "Do you have any security cameras?" I asked.

"Are you wondering if someone snuck in here?" Ava asked.

That did sound better. "Sure," I lied.

"We don't have any security cameras in here, or anywhere else on the island," Kildare said. He pointed to Ashley. "Her choice, not mine."

The bazillionaire cringed. "I don't look good on video."

Hank transferred the photos from the submarine, then brought up the images on two large monitors. Rosa pointed at the picture showing the base of the pipe. "This clearly isn't natural. You were right, Jack. This was definitely sabotage."

Would a bow have been appropriate? I settled on a nod and thanked her. At least someone was willing to recognize my work.

Ashley moved to the screen. Over her shoulder, she said, "SEAL?"

"You think a seal could've done that?" I asked.

Matt leaned in and quietly explained. "She's asking for input from Kildare, Jack."

"Looks like a standard underwater demolition job to me," Kildare said.

"I still don't get it," Ava said. "What's the motive, you know?" She turned to Rosa. "Who would want you to fail?"

The engineer dropped into a chair with her back to the screens. She spun around twice, then stopped and rubbed her chin. "My grad school professor? He despises me because I'm brighter than he is. And my older sister. She has always been jealous."

Kildare coughed. "I think she means to ask who might want this project to fail. Not you in particular."

"Oh. Oil companies."

"Do they know about it?" Matt asked.

"Sure," Rosa said.

"Other inventors, maybe," Ashley added.

"Who else?" Hank asked.

I looked down at the still water surrounding the submarine. Ashley was innocent; I was certain of that now. But what if it was someone on the island? A housekeeper tired of the Hawkings? Was the chef so annoyed by the demanding bazillionaire and her gluten-free son that he'd bring down their thirty-million-dollar project? No, that was a stretch.

The logical culprits were those boatbuilding dentists. "What about the islanders?" I said. "Ben and his friends. Are they still here?"

Ashley looked to Kildare. "They're hanging around for the party," he said. "They're anchored at the southern end of the island, camping on the beach."

"They've already admitted they don't want you here," Matt added.

"But would they really go to such lengths?" Ashley asked.

"Depths," Hank noted with a smile.

No one laughed.

"They'd need a submarine to get down there," I said.

"Like the *Nautilus Redux*," Ava said.

"Yes," Hank said, "but the TOES broke down weeks ago. The *Nautilus* wasn't even here yet. It was still back in my lab."

"So where else could one find a submarine like that?" Matt asked.

"A research facility," Rosa suggested. "Maybe one of the universities?"

"I'll find out," Kildare declared.

"Good," Ashley said. She held her hands behind her back, just like her son. "While you're doing that, why don't the rest of us head back to the house? It's been a long morning. I think we could all use some rest."

• • •

Maybe it was the long trip from New York. Or my lack of sleep the night before. Or the absurdly stressful flirtation with death down in the deep ocean. But apparently I was exhausted. I slept for two hours that afternoon, then spent the evening watching a movie in Ava's room while she read about the TOES. Matt was studying again. His online test was Thursday, but he was cramming like he only had an hour to go. And Hank was working late with Rosa in the laboratory again.

The next morning, I woke up feeling like a completely new person, and my mood further improved when Ashley led Matt, Ava, and me outside, where four stunningly beautiful all-terrain vehicles awaited us. "Well," Ashley said. "What do you think?"

"These are for us?" I asked, my voice quivering with joy.

Ashley laughed. "For Google's sake, no! Of course not. These are all for Steven. Do you think he'll like them?"

"You got him four ATVs for his birthday?" I asked.

"I suppose I should have gotten five, to include Albert's daughter." She stared at the vehicles as if she were actually questioning her decision. "But maybe we just won't tell her, okay? Ah, here he is now. Good morning, Steven."

He yawned. "They're electric," he said.

"Yes, but don't worry, they're still powerful," she said.

"You and your new friends could use them to explore the island a little."

"Sure," Steven said. "Go ahead," he said to us, "pick one."

I approached the one on the far left. The body gleamed. The tires shined. The rubber handlebar grips smelled amazing. I swung my leg over the seat. Kildare hurried out of the house and tossed us each a helmet, then said something to Steven about how he'd thrown some gear into the compartments under the seats. Matt didn't wait for further confirmation. He cranked the throttle and sped away. Ava went next. I flipped the switch to start the electric engine. Nothing happened. I tried again. Still nothing. The motor in Steven's ATV, meanwhile, was whirring beautifully.

"That one must be dead, Jack," Kildare said. "I must not have charged it fully. Steven, you want to let him go with you?"

"Can't he just wait? It's my birthday!"

"Be nice to your guest, Steven," Ashley suggested.

The worst part of this deal was not that I had to share with Steven Hawking. Or the look of complete disgust on his face when he scooted forward to make room. No. The worst part was when I realized there were no handles to hold in back. But I wasn't going to wrap my arms around his waist. No

way. Not in a billion years. So I gritted my teeth and grabbed his shoulders.

The back of the ATV swung wide as we tore down the path after the others. The engine whined like a million buzzing bees, and we followed Matt and Ava as they veered off onto the grass. Surprisingly, Steven wasn't a bad driver. "Have you done this before?" I yelled. He didn't answer. We were coming to the top of the first hill. The path split. When we slowed, Matt broke off to the right, where a series of flat and wide green and gray hills rolled down toward the southern end of the island.

Steven stopped. "Where are they going?" he asked.

"I don't know."

But I could have guessed. And I didn't have to tell Steven to follow them. He accelerated so hard that I nearly fell off the back. "Too fast for you?" he shouted.

Yes, a little, but I'd never admit to that. As we sped down, I gripped his shoulders harder. The house was far up the hill, back over my right shoulder, at the top of the cliffs. That was the island's highest point. From there it basically sloped down to the southern end, which was a mix of low cliffs and small coves.

We came down over the last hill and slowed as we followed a path along the cliff. Matt and Ava rolled to a stop. Steven did the same, and I climbed off the ATV. We stood at one end of the wide, crescent-shaped cove. The rock walls were high on either end but sloped down to the middle, where a path opened onto the wide beach. *Ohana* and *Niu* were anchored just outside the opening to the cove, rising and falling gently as wide waves rolled beneath them. The laboratory dock was barely visible in the distance. Ben stood watching from the big boat, but the others were in the water, straddling surfboards. A thick wave rolled beneath them and toward the shore.

David turned his large wooden board, paddled, and sprang to his feet as a wave caught up to him from behind. After a second he shuffled his feet to the back, swung the board to his right, in our direction, and stepped back to the middle as he cruised down the glassy wave with the bright white foam chasing him. What he was doing didn't look like surfing. It reminded me of dancing.

"There's Maya," Ava said, pointing.

Maya's board was green and white, with a large pink flower near the nose, and it was two-thirds the size of her uncle's ride. She was already on her knees when she started paddling, and while she didn't whip the board around as much as David, her ride was just as long and smooth. She barely moved at all as the wave carried her along its slowly breaking face. Then, when the last of the wave was breaking, she rushed forward to the nose and stopped with her toes at the edge and her arms held high overhead. The other surfers cheered and whistled.

Matt stared in wonder. "That was amazing."

"She's pretty good," Steven admitted.

"Who's pretty good?" Matt asked.

Ava pointed down at the water. Maya was knee-paddling back out over the tops of the incoming waves. "The girl," Ava said. "What were you talking about?"

"Oh, I was watching the waves. Did you notice how they bend into a semicircle as they flow into the cove?" He put his hand on my shoulder and pointed. "That's the island slowing down the edges. And when each wave gets close to the shore, the center stands up and slows as it feels the bottom. Amazing. Look!" I followed his hand as it moved along with the rolling wave. "There it goes again. Completely mesmerizing, right?"

I had a question, but Ava asked it for me. "Since when do you know so much about surfing?"

"I don't know anything about surfing," Matt responded. "That's just basic physics. Waves are waves, whether they're traveling through empty space"—he pointed directly above us—"or rolling into shore from the deep blue sea. Now, should we head down there and ask a few questions?"

"Don't tell me you're playing detectives again," Steven said. "Is that honestly why we're here?"

Matt shrugged. "They have a clear motive."

"Can't it wait?" Steven asked. "They've already said they're coming to my party. You can ask them later."

Ava responded in what sounded like Chinese.

Then my sister switched to English, adding, "That's a quote from Sun Tzu."

Steven replied in Chinese, started our ATV, and sped down the path without me.

"What did he say?" I asked.

The corner of Ava's mouth peaked into a frustrated sneer. She crossed her arms and shifted her weight to her right side. "He said I made up the quote."

"Did you?" Matt asked.

She shrugged. "How was I supposed to know he speaks Mandarin?"

123

Ava sped after Steven, and Matt made room for me on the back. We followed the path down around the low cliffs to the beach, cutting through bushes. The branches scratched against the sides of my legs and ankles, but it didn't bother Matt, so I wasn't going to say anything. When we stopped on the sand, Steven was leaning back against the front of his ATV, watching the islanders surf.

I waved to them.

"Tried that," he said. "It's like they're pretending we're not even here."

"Maybe we should go to them," Ava suggested.

"Huh?"

"If they're not coming to us, let's go to them."

Apparently she'd worn a bathing suit, and now she tossed her shirt and shorts onto the sand, pulled off her shoes, propped her phone up on the dashboard of her ATV, and started toward the water. "What? It's Hawaii. Of course I wore a suit."

"Wait!" Matt said. "You're swimming out there? I can't let you—"

"Since when do you get to let me?"

"I'm the oldest, and Hank would want—"

"Stop worrying about what Hank wants, Matt," Ava snapped.

My brother mumbled. Steven beamed, thrilled to see us fighting.

I looked out at the water. "What about the sharks?"

"They wouldn't be surfing if there were sharks, right?" Matt asked.

"No," Steven said, "they'd probably surf anyway. But there aren't any sharks."

"How do you know?"

He pulled out his phone, thumb-typed, then turned the screen to face us. I had to shield my eyes because of the glare. But I could see a map of the island and the surrounding water, with several red dots on the far side—the same app we saw in the laboratory. "See? The sharks are over there. Not here."

"Great," Ava said. "Then I'm going to swim out and say hello. Anyone coming with me?"

Steven lifted the seat of his ATV and removed goggles and swim fins from the compartment. "I should warn you," he said. "I was nationally ranked when I was eight years old."

"Are there extras?" I asked.

He pointed to the compartment. Then he tossed his shirt and shoes aside and raced for the water. "You coming?" I asked Matt.

My brother unzipped his backpack and removed his laptop. "I'll just study."

"Now? On the beach?"

"Yes! Okay?"

I didn't mean to laugh. But I didn't know how else to react. "Okay," I added with shrug.

My brother's face turned red. "You don't get it, do you? This test . . . you wouldn't understand." Too frustrated to finish, Matt turned his back to me, sat against his ATV, and focused on his screen.

He was right. Sometimes, I really didn't understand.

By the time I'd reached the edge of the water, Ava and Steven were already ducking beneath the waves. My sister didn't swim in races or anything. She'd never been on a team. But every time we jumped in the pool at the Y, someone would tell her she was a natural, and when we rode the subway out to Rockaway Beach in the summer, she'd dart around in the waves like a dolphin.

Hank marveled at her skill when he caught us swimming in the dive tank at his lab one time. He'd been angry at first, or as angry as Hank gets, which is more of a simmer than a boil. But he was quickly distracted by Ava's fish-like skills. "You kick like a porpoise," he said, "using your body instead of your feet. Where'd you learn that?" She said she didn't know, which was probably true. Unfortunately, Ava didn't know much at all about the first four years of her life. Heat and water and music, she'd say. That was all she could remember. And now, watching her kick out through the waves, past the avalanche of foam to where the water was a glassy green and blue, you would've thought she was raised under the sea with King Triton and his daughters.

I stopped watching and plunged in after them. The fins helped. I dog-paddled and kicked between the waves, diving like a seal when they roared close. I thought I was doing just fine. But the waves were growing. The walls of crumbling whitewater were getting taller and faster. My good-luck charm was all wound up and digging into my neck. After what felt like ten minutes, I still wasn't making any progress.

After popping up from under one wave, I surfaced just in time to see another large swell rushing forward like an avalanche. I tried to dive under. The churning water grabbed me and flipped me backward, whipping me around like I was a dirty T-shirt inside a washing machine. When I finally came up for air again, I gulped down a mouthful of seawater. The next wave was already rushing at me. Ava and Steven were gone. I turned to look back at the shore. Neither Matt nor the ATVs were anywhere close. And I was close to the cliffs. A current must have swept me down to the other end of the cove.

The whitewater smacked me in the back of the head. Then I was under again, tumbling, only this time I hadn't thought to take a breath. I felt something brush across my back. My first thought? Shark. And not just any shark. At that moment, I was absolutely certain I was being pursued by a prehistoric megalodon. I even pictured the news stories that would follow. They'd only mention me briefly before lingering on my poor siblings and Hank and their loss. One or two news anchors would probably wonder aloud, almost hopefully, whether the tragedy would inspire my siblings to write another book of poetry. *The Heartbroken Orphans*, maybe? A book like that would sell a warehouse full of copies. And I wouldn't be around to enjoy any of the royalties. I wouldn't be around for anything. Out of breath, out of energy, and who knows how far from the surface, I was certain that I was finished.

9

MRS. WINTERBOTTOM'S MOLARS

SO HERE'S THE THING ABOUT SHARKS. THEY DON'T grab you by the forearm and pull you to the surface, then lay you on your back with their hands across your chest and keep you afloat so you can catch your breath. People do that sort of thing. Especially those who care about you and don't want to see you drown or get hurt or even suffer. Still, it took me a few seconds to realize that I hadn't been bumped by a fierce fish. I'd been rescued by Hank, and I started to thank him. He turned me back over onto my stomach. "Later," he said. "The next wave's coming. Deep breath, deep dive."

My lungs burned, but I sucked in some air and let Hank pull me under. We popped back up when the wave passed, and the next one looked half the size. "You okay?" he asked. He signaled someone. Matt was treading water nearby, watching me with concern. But Hank wasn't calling to him. David was riding toward us on the huge wooden board, lying on his stomach. He sat up and pulled at the board so it was nearly vertical. The whitewater surged past him and he stayed in place. We ducked under the small wave. When I surfaced, David was waiting in the swirling but mostly calm water between the swells. "Get on," he said. His emotionless tone told me this was an order, not an invitation. He glanced down at Hank and Matt.

"We'll be fine," Hank said. "Go ahead."

I climbed up onto the huge surfboard and lay on my stomach with my head near the nose. David tapped my feet; I bent my legs at the knees and lifted my feet up in the air to give him more room. Then he turned the board into the next wave and started paddling. Each time the whitewater rushed at us he told me to hold on, and each time we plunged through and, after a pause, resumed moving. After five waves, we made it past the break and accelerated up and over the incoming swells instead of punching through them. A minute later we were pulling alongside *Ohana*. Steven and Ava were already standing on the platform with Maya and the old man, Ben.

129

Maya offered her hand, but I climbed up on my own. For about the fiftieth time I tried to thank David, but he was gone, paddling back to the waves.

"You made him miss a good set," Maya explained.

"He'll get over it," Ben said. "There are always more waves."

Hank and Matt swam up to us. My brother kind of flailed at the water, like he was fighting an invisible merman, but our mentor's stroke was long and easy. When he pulled himself out of the water, Hank wasn't even short of breath. "You're okay, Jack?"

"Yes, thank you." I looked at Matt. "Done studying?"

He patted me on the side of the shoulder. "I was worried when you swam out there. You're not exactly a fish. Sorry, but I had to call Hank."

"Good move," Maya said.

That stung a little.

"Those waves were big, Jack," Ava added. "That could have happened to anyone."

"That was nothing," Steven said. "I've swum in much larger surf."

"You know the water, Dr. Witherspoon," Ben said.

"Hank, please. And yes, I do. A little. We summered on the ocean when I was a kid," Hank said. "Worked as a lifeguard, too, but I didn't last long. The waves and weather were too interesting. I couldn't focus on the swimmers. Also, the other lifeguards used to steal my sandwiches. Now," he said, turning to Ava and me, "what are you doing out here?"

"I was going to ask them the same question," Ben said.

My attempt at an answer turned into a garbled cough. Ava and Hank leaned in to check on me, but I waved them off.

"We were hoping to talk to you," Ava said.

"Why?" Maya asked.

I looked to Ava to answer. She widened her eyes and leaned forward. My turn, apparently. I coughed again. "Well," I began, "because . . ."

"Oh, I know!" Hank said. "You're still wondering whether they sabotaged the TOES."

None of us had ever accused Hank of being a good detective.

"David's a dentist," Ben said. "Teeth, not toes. You're thinking of podiatry."

"The Thermal Ocean Energy System," Ava explained. "Or TOES for short."

"The underwater electricity plant," Maya said.

"Yes, yes, I know," Ben said. "I was joking."

"My grandfather has a unique sense of humor," Maya replied in a flat tone.

"You think we're the ones who broke it?" Ben asked.

"You'd have to secure a submarine and find someone to operate it," Hank explained. "Then there's the not-so-small matter of getting hold of enough explosives to destroy the bottom of the pipe. You don't just pick up these kinds of things on your own."

"My son and his friends are very resourceful," Ben said. "They could learn, I'm sure."

"You're not helping, Grandfather," Maya said.

"We both know they'd never do anything like that, Maya. So we might as well be honest."

My breath had finally come back. "You want it to fail, though, right?"

"Sure, we all do," Maya said. "Or at least fail here. The TOES is a brilliant concept. We just don't want it on Nihoa."

"You mean you don't want us here," Steven snapped.

They didn't answer.

Now that my head felt like all the water had drained out, I realized something. In this one episode of *Duck Detective*, the feathered sleuth suspects a certain troublemaking goat of stealing a neighborhood boy's bicycle, only to find out that the animal in question was with two dozen of his bleating buddies when the crime took place. The goat had an alibi. What about the islanders? Sure, they had a motive. No one was even denying that. But if they had solid alibis, then we might have to drop them as suspects. "Where were you the day before the demonstration?" I asked.

"That's actually a good question, Jack," Hank said.

Was this really so surprising?

"Why?" Ben asked.

"That's when the system stopped working properly."

"Were you here on the island?" Ava pressed.

Maya said she wasn't sure. Ben stared at the sky as if he

133

were reading the clouds. Then one of his eyes closed. Was he calling on some ancient god for knowledge? Saying a prayer to help him devise a decent excuse for his son? His left cheek bulged slightly. Then he sighed and smiled. "Ah, got it. A little sesame seed has been stuck in my teeth since yesterday. Now, you asked where we were the day before the demonstration?" I nodded. "What day was that, exactly?"

Squinting, Hank tapped his fingers on his chin. "Two weeks ago yesterday."

"A Tuesday?"

"Yes, Tuesday!" Steven said, fiercely annoyed.

Hank paused, then nodded with certainty. "That's right."

Ben crossed to the other side of the boat, opened a hatch, pulled out a backpack, and removed a worn leather notebook.

"That's the appointment book," Maya explained. "My uncle does most of the dental work, but Grandfather still runs the business."

Hank was reaching into the back of his mouth with his thumb. "I sometimes wonder about my wisdom teeth. I never had them removed, and I can't help but ask myself sometimes if I would be wiser without them. Or maybe less so?"

I caught Matt wriggling his jaw. Asking himself the same question, I'm sure.

"You're too young for wisdom teeth," Ben said to my brother. Then he tapped the page, waved me over, and pointed to the day in question. A single patient's name was written there, with arrows above and below. Apparently she'd swallowed up the whole day. "This was a long one," Ben said.

His handwriting was scrawled, but legible. "Who's Mrs. Winterbottom?" I asked.

"An English lady," Ben said. "She's one of our best clients because she lives in the Princeville Hotel on the north shore of Kauai."

Living in a hotel was basically my dream. When the three of us first got away from Alice and Bob, our last set of foster parents, who believed boxed macaroni and cheese was the perfect breakfast, lunch, and dinner, I actually begged Matt and Ava to avoid looking for a normal place to live. There was a perfectly good hotel with reasonable long-term rates not too far away. It had a pool, a game room, free breakfast in the morning, and, of course, housecleaning. We wouldn't have needed to make our beds, let alone hang up our towels. But no. They said that was irresponsible. Unnatural—that was Matt's word. So they found us our small, overpriced apartment in Brooklyn.

But anyway. Back to Mrs. Winterbottom. "What does living in a hotel have to do with her teeth?"

135

"She has tea and cookies four times a day, smokes cigarettes constantly, and spends most of her time lounging in the pool. The sugar and smoke would have been enough, but chlorine is no friend to teeth, either, so hers are positively rotten," Ben said. "Which is great for us."

"It's true," Maya added. "I've seen her molars. They're as yellow as egg yolks."

Ben tapped the book again. "That morning, David had a six-hour-long procedure replacing several of her molars. Derek assists him, so he would've been there, too. And Betsy, our dental hygienist, had seven cleanings. There's no way any of them could have gotten out here to Nihoa in time to sabotage the TOES."

"What about you?"

"I was golfing."

"You're sure?" I asked.

"He literally golfs every day when we're not on this boat," Maya replied.

I held up my index finger. "So, wait, let me just go over this again—"

"I think we've been helpful enough," Ben said with a fake smile. He went to put away the book, then glanced out at David, Betsy, and Derek on their boards. "I don't think my son and the others would be quite so friendly, considering that you're accusing us of a crime."

Matt and Hank stared at me angrily. Now I was the bad guy?

"We're sorry," Hank said. "You're absolutely right."

Steven pointed to the water. "Can we please just swim ashore now? This is absurd."

"What if he took a plane?" I asked.

Ava snapped her fingers. "Or a helicopter?"

"Really, that's enough," Hank said. Again he apologized.

Maya was watching something over my shoulder. A wave? A shark? I turned to see a small boat rounding the southern corner of the cove. The bow was high out of the water. "Is that your mom?" I asked Steven.

He squinted. As the boat roared closer, the driver's visor and dark glasses came into view. "No, it's my babysitter," he said with a frustrated sigh.

"Your babysitter?"

"Kildare," he explained. "He doesn't like me swimming out here."

"How does he know we're out here?"

"He knows everything that happens on this island."

Ava scanned the sky. Looking for drones, most likely. Hank was studying the coast with the same intensity. Were there cameras hidden in the rocks?

Kildare shut off the engine. *Vader*'s bow dipped, its stern rose, and the boat drifted straight up to *Ohana*. I asked Maya to apologize to her uncle for making him miss those

137

waves. She smiled but said nothing, and the silence that followed lasted for about a million years. I wanted to make sure she was coming to the party. But the question was trapped at the bottom of an ocean trench in the middle of my chest.

"See you tonight?" Ava asked her.

Maya looked over at her grandfather before responding. "Yes, we will."

Ben was stretching his shoulders, preparing to dive into the water, when he turned and addressed me directly. "I'd offer more help," he said. "But I can't say that I want you to succeed. Whoever is sabotaging the TOES is doing us a service," he said.

I thought little Steven Hawking was going to be upset. Maybe he'd kick or scream or cry. Instead, he offered the old man the same ice-cold smile. "Understood, Ben."

"You can call me Dr. Adrian."

"I can call you whatever I like," Steven said, and then he hopped down into the boat.

The rest of us followed, and Kildare piloted us back to shore, expertly riding the whitewater of an oncoming wave. I stood with my back to the bow, watching the strange crew of surfing dentists. Yes, they had a motive. But their alibis were impeccable. Still, if it wasn't them, then who in the world was sabotaging the project? A motive and an alibi were only the start. As Hank pointed out, the person would also need to be remarkably resourceful—skilled with explosives, submarines, and more. I turned to the beach and watched as the one person on the island who met those qualifications steered *Vader* onto the sand.

10
THE GLIMMER
AND THE GULL

O

UTSIDE THE FRONT DOOR OF THE HOUSE, THE air-conditioning king reclined in an enormous wooden beach chair with his face to the sun. His brightly colored shirt was unbuttoned. His straw hat was tilted back. A tall, sweating glass of water rested on the top of his stomach. His sandals were leather, his board shorts long and blue, and he was so completely absorbed that I couldn't help wondering if he was using photosynthesis. Was he eating sunlight? Was that even possible? I'd have to ask Hank later, in private.

Beside him, the robot held an electric fan. The king didn't react to the sound of our ATVs roaring up the hill. He didn't move when we shut them off and our footsteps crunched on the gravel path. He didn't flinch when Hank coughed.

Twice.

"He looks dead," Ava said.

"Maybe he's meditating," Matt suggested.

"Sunbathing is a terrible habit, kids," Hank warned. "Don't start."

Kildare grumbled something in reply. Unfortunately, the SEAL insisted on escorting us all the way back to the house, so I still hadn't told the others about my new theory.

The robot spun abruptly and aimed the fan in our direction. The air had to be twenty degrees cooler. I closed my eyes and leaned into it as the king popped up out of his seat. He removed the tiniest headphones I'd ever seen and proclaimed, "Welcome!"

"This isn't your house," Steven said. "What are you doing with the HR-5?"

"The robot? Oh, nothing. Nothing. And no, it isn't my house. You're right. But your mother has told me on numerous occasions that her home is our home. Or maybe that was my sister? She has a positively majestic ranch in Wyoming. Very cool there in the mountains. No need for air-conditioning, though, so naturally I don't really like the place." He squinted. "So, what have you been up to? I meant to ask about your little submarine jaunt yesterday. You were the one who joined Ashley, right?" He jabbed me in the chest with one of his stubby fingers. "Any interesting creatures?"

"A whole bunch of bristlemouths," I said.

"Is that a kind of toothbrush?" he asked. "It's tragic how

141

much we're polluting our planet. First plastic bottles, now toothbrushes. That's why I love what your mother is doing, Steven. Saving the world."

"Whatever," Steven said. "I have work to do."

Kildare followed the prince inside.

The king snapped his fingers at the robot. "This way, this way, my silicon-brained friend. Do any of these people really look all that overheated?" He turned to me. "Robots, right? So smart in the movies, but in the real world they're as dumb as"—he kicked the gravel path—"rocks!" He took a long drink of water. "How about you four? Lemonade? Maybe a sandwich? Go in and help yourself. The chefs are whipping up some delightful little concoctions for tonight's party, and they don't mind at all if you waltz right in there and test them. Try the marinated olives. Or the brownies. Not together, though. Terrible combination. Go on, go on, really. I'd join you, but I need at least another hour of this photogenic recuperation." He struck a boxing pose and jabbed Matt in the arm. "Know what I mean?"

Matt rubbed his shoulder and glanced at Hank. He probably wanted approval to punch back, but Hank didn't notice. His brain appeared to have jumped on a flight to another continent. Sometimes I wondered if he was really thinking deeply during moments like that, or if his brain was temporarily frozen like a buggy smartphone. I was tempted to snap my fingers in front of his face.

142

"Thanks for the suggestion," Ava said. "We'll give it a try."

"Hank, are you there?" the air-conditioning king asked. "Mr. Witherspoon? While the children are inside I would absolutely love to bounce a few rather stellar ideas off your noble brain."

Our mentor blinked. "Yes, of course!" Hank answered with a smile. "Later. At the party. Enjoy your photons, sir."

The second we were through the door, all four of us exhaled.

"That guy . . ." Matt began.

"Look," Hank said, "I'm going back out to the lab to do a little more work on the TOES, but maybe it would be a good idea if the three of you took some downtime?" He was talking to me in particular. This probably wasn't a good time to tell him I wanted to follow Kildare.

"I need to study anyway," Matt said.

This had to stop. Really. "You just were studying," I pointed out. "On the beach. In Hawaii."

Gritting his teeth, Matt replied, "Because I—"

"Studying is a great idea," Hank said. "Why don't you each catch up on your assignments for school?" There was no way I was going to do homework now. And Hank must have figured that out. "Jack?"

"Yes, homework. Totally."

143

"Good."

"And Hank?"

"Yes, Jack?

"Thanks for, you know . . ."

He smiled, nodded, and walked back down the hill.

Matt hurried up the stairs, and I expected Ava to do the same. Instead, she lifted her hand to her chin and pointed in the direction of the kitchen. "Brownies?"

"Absolutely!"

As we walked to the kitchen, I felt lighter. Optimistic. And not because of the luscious smells of the freshly baked treats. No, I was thinking of how much I loved these moments when my siblings revealed themselves to be actual kids—when Matt sat next to me and pretended not to be interested in whatever game I was watching on television, then fist-pumped after a touchdown or a basket. Or when my sister skipped a chance to tinker with a robot so she could gobble some brownies. Sure, they were geniuses. They were more focused and resourceful than most adults. But these moments proved they were like me, too. You know. Normal.

Plus, this would be a good time to tell her my theory about Kildare.

Then she yanked at my shirt. "Why are you smiling? We have work to do."

She was hurrying along the wall, back to the front door. Away from the kitchen.

"But, the brownies . . ."

Her tongue dropped out of her mouth in frustration. "I thought it was obvious that was a ruse," she said.

"Right," I lied. "It was."

"Good. Follow me."

The smell was so strong I could practically taste the chocolate. We totally could've grabbed a treat and then followed her plan. But Ava had that look. Sometimes it's not easy to pinpoint. There's just a weird glimmer to her eyes. At other times, the creases in her forehead will transform into this V-shaped curve that looks a little like a seagull in flight. Now she had both going—the glimmer and the gull. "What's up?" I whispered. "Listen, I want to talk to you about Kildare. I wonder if he's the one . . . wait, where are we going?"

She lifted her finger to her lips, opened a door near the entrance, pulled me in after her, and closed it behind us. Inside, it was pitch-black. "So, uh, what are we doing?"

"Give me your necklace."

"It's not a necklace."

"Fine. Your good luck charm." I handed it over. She activated the flashlight app on her phone and passed it to me. "Hold it like this," she said, aiming it at the good luck

145

charm. She opened the lid, then tried to pry out the photo of Mr. Winkles with her fingernail.

"Careful!" I was starting to like the cat.

"Shhh."

I hated being shushed. And her shush was louder than my question, so what was the point? She reached into her back pocket and removed a small plastic vial. "Put out your hand," she ordered. Then she popped open the cap and poured the contents of the vial into my open palm. Several tiny screwdrivers spilled out. She picked one that looked like it had a flat head but wasn't much bigger than a sewing needle. Then she eased it around the edges of Mr. Winkle's portrait.

"If you like it so much, you could probably just ask him for one of your own," I said.

"I don't want the cat." The photo popped out. "I want this."

She tilted the good luck charm into the light of the phone. The interior was green and crossed with miniature silver and bronze lines. A few black plastic squares sprouted thin wires that looked like little legs. A small circular battery sat in the middle. I'd seen hundreds of these things before on our kitchen table. I probably cleaned one out of the way every morning just to clear a spot for my cereal. I even knew that what I was looking at was basically the brains of almost every piece of modern electronics, from a television remote control to a computer.

But of course I couldn't remember what they were called. "That's a . . . a . . . whatchamacallit."

"A circuit board," she said.

Yes. Right. I knew that. But it still didn't make sense. "Why is Mr. Winkles hiding a circuit board?"

"Because this isn't a good-luck charm," Ava said. "It's a tracking device. Kildare gave you this so he'd know where you are at all times. That's probably why he wants us to carry our phones, too."

"I don't get it."

"That app Steven showed us—the one we saw in the lab—it doesn't just track the sharks," she said. "It tracks people, too. Look, I'll show you." She opened the same program on her phone that Steven had shown me on the beach. The red dots were still circling in the same place. But then she tapped the screen, brought up a menu, and switched the view. A small window appeared, asking for a password. She carefully typed a series of letters and numbers, and the window disappeared.

"How'd you know the password?"

Ava winked. "I have my ways."

Now we were looking at the same map, but with green dots. Ava touched the screen with her thumb and index fingers and spread them apart several times, zooming in. She moved in on the house.

Two green dots blinked near the door. "That's us?" I asked.

"That's us."

"Why's he tracking us?"

"That's what we're going to find out, Jack," she said. "You said yourself he's a suspect. But before we figure out whether he's behind this, we need to get him off our trail."

The smart thing to do would've been to open the door only a crack and look out first. Then we would've known if someone was coming. But I wasn't really thinking, and I nearly knocked over a member of the kitchen staff.

148

"Excuse me! Sorry," I said. The woman stared back. Her hair was long and black, and her skin was far too pale for someone living in Hawaii. "See, Ava, I told you that closet wasn't the entrance to a magical world of talking bears." Then, to the woman, I added, "Kids and their imaginations, you know?"

The woman held a silver tray. Ignoring me, Ava pointed to a tall glass of lemonade. A sprig of mint leaned against the rim. "Is that for the king?"

"Yes," the woman said.

Her accent was unusual. Normally Ava picked these things up first. "Are you from Eastern Europe?" I asked. "Lithuania?"

"No, Santa Monica," she said. My embarrassed sister covered her eyes. The woman leaned forward and whispered, "Don't tell anyone, but we call him the walrus."

I laughed harder than I should have.

"Can we bring that out to him?" Ava asked.

"Be my guest," she said. "When I delivered the last glass, he belched and I nearly threw up. I actually felt the burp particles hit my face." She touched her pale cheek gently with her free hand, as if to check if the traces of his belch were still there.

"We'll be careful," Ava said, taking the tray.

As Ava moved to the door, my brain was swinging in a different direction. Were burp particles real? And if so, were they called "burpicles"? If they did exist, and no one had studied them yet, then maybe I could be the one who introduced them to the world. I could make a major scientific discovery before my brother and sister. The research community would call me the father of burpicles. The professor of belches. The king of mouth monsoons. I jotted down the word and a question mark in my little notebook.

149

Ava snapped her index finger against the page. "What's with you and that notebook? Planning to tell another blogger about this adventure, too?"

"You have no proof that was me," I said. "Maybe it was you. Or Matt." I pointed to the lemonade. "Why are we serving him?"

She tossed me the circuit board underhand. "So he can keep this for us."

"Why would he do that?"

"He won't know," she said. "While I'm delivering this refreshing drink, you're going to slip that under the brim of his straw hat."

Before I could protest, she backed out through the door. Outside, the robot directed its fans at us immediately.

"Your lemonade, sir," Ava said.

"Thank you!" the king replied. "Thank you, thank you!" He sat up and sipped. Then he chewed on the mint leaf, removed it from his mouth, and pointed it at Ava. "You're one of the smart ones, right? The robot girl?"

"Ava," she reminded him. "Not the robot girl."

151

"Right, right. Well, anyway, I was sitting here, sweating, and I had a pretty good idea for a new invention. A brilliant one, really." He leaned back and sipped his lemonade again, then closed his eyes.

"Go on," Ava said, glaring first at me, then at the hat on the table beside him.

"Well, how about an air-conditioning robot? It could just roll around and follow you everywhere to keep you cool."

I hadn't moved. An air-conditioning robot? Would that work? And would it store ice pops or delicious bottles of lemonade in a little freezer in its stomach? If so, I wanted one now.

A tiny pebble pinged off the side of my head.

Ava held a second piece of gravel on the pad of her right thumb, with her index finger ready to fire.

Message received.

The king was rambling on about his robot, and how everyone could have one of their own and nobody would ever have to be hot again. I edged closer, reached out for the hat, then yanked back my hand as he blindly grabbed out for his headwear. He pressed the inside of his hat against his forehead and repeatedly ran it from his brow to the top of his dripping head, mopping up the sweat. Then he placed the hat back down on the table and started on about how there could even be all-terrain models that followed you while you were hiking. I reached forward and slipped the tiny electronic square under the hat band. The elastic was damp and hot from his head sweat.

"I think it's a brilliant idea," Ava said.

Then she turned to me and stuck her tongue out of the corner of her mouth and crossed her eyes.

"I'm full of brilliant ideas," he said. "That's why they call me the king."

11
A PARTY FOR A PRINCE

L IVING ON YOUR OWN AS A TWELVE-YEAR-OLD ISN'T all chocolate chips and rainbows. Sure, you set your own rules. But you also have to feed yourself and make sure your clothes don't stink and remember to buy toilet paper when you run low so you're not stuck using the pages of some sappy book of orphan poetry. You don't hang out with too many kids your age, either, so you don't get invited to many birthday parties. Honestly, the last one I attended was for a neighborhood kid when I was ten years old and living with two other foster brats in a nearly nice house in New Jersey. The piñata was enormous, but the parents were health fanatics, so it was packed with strawberries instead of candy, and when the birthday boy knocked it open he just kept whacking it over and over. The inside turned into this bright red gushy mush of berries that looked way too much like the guts of a real animal, not a cardboard

153

donkey, and a few of the kids legitimately freaked out. I'm talking hair-pulling, red-faced, tear-streaming shrieking fits.

Hopefully this wasn't going to be that kind of party.

I picked a nice silk bow tie, a yellow one with miniature pineapples that Hank had given me for the trip. My white shirt and khakis looked about right, but the jacket was too much. At the last second I took it off and tossed it on my bed.

Ava had been knocking on my door for a while, telling me to hurry up. But the party had just started, and I liked being fashionably late. Plus, I was nervous. After planting the tracking device on the king, we'd rushed to Matt's room to tell him about Kildare. Then the three of us hurried to tell Hank, but he was still out at the lab with Rosa. Part of me had been hoping Hank would tell us to leave the whole Kildare problem up to him. And maybe he still would. But for now it was up to us.

Once I finished with my hair, I let her in. She pointed to the Mr. Winkles charm on my desk. "Bring that," she said. "We don't want Kildare getting suspicious." Then she glanced at my shoes. I was proud—they were so perfectly polished I could almost see my reflection.

"What?" I asked.

"Nothing."

"Tell me."

"Too formal. I think Maya would dig the casual look."

Reaching back onto the desk, I grabbed something to throw at her. Unfortunately, it was a tissue, and it drifted to the floor before traveling two feet. I closed the door in her smiling face and informed her that I would need another minute. She was right about the shoes. I switched into the high-tops. They didn't look quite right, either, though, so I replaced the laces with the bright yellow SpiderStretch brand I'd grabbed from the lab. Then I caught up to Ava at the bottom of the stairs. "Where's Matt?" I asked. "Still studying?"

"No, I'm right here," he said. He was waiting on the first floor, wearing a blue blazer over the second ugliest Hawaiian shirt I'd ever seen. The sleeves of the jacket ended halfway up his forearms.

"Are those supposed to be palm trees?" I asked.

He shrugged. "I don't know. Hank gave it to me earlier. It's one of his old ones."

"And the jacket?"

"It's mine. Why?" he asked, extending his arms. "Too small?"

I didn't answer.

"Did you find anything out?" Ava asked him.

"Nothing much," Matt whispered. "Looks like he was a SEAL for six years, and before that he was a national badminton champion at the Naval Academy."

155

"They have badminton in the Navy?" I asked.

"Wonderful sport," Matt replied. "Requires phenomenal agility and hand-eye coordination. What did you guys find out?"

"I did some research on the SEAL program," Ava said. "They're trained in underwater demolition and piloting underwater vehicles. But they have a pretty serious code of honor, too, which doesn't fit with the whole saboteur theory."

"Interesting," Matt said. "You, Jack?"

I shrugged. "Sorry, I was getting dressed."

And I wasn't sure that any of these new facts about Kildare really added up to much. Maybe Ashley had asked him to track us to keep us out of trouble. Or danger. I mean, I'd almost drowned. Then again, he wasn't around to save me. He'd only rushed onto the scene after Hank had pulled me from the water.

In one way he was the perfect suspect. He knew how to blow stuff up underwater. He knew how to drive a submarine. But what was his motive? Did he have something against Ashley or Rosa? Was someone paying him? Plenty of people forget their codes of honor when there's cash involved.

Matt checked his watch. "Let's go," he said. "I don't like being late."

The pale-skinned, black-haired kitchen staffer crossed from the kitchen to a sliding door leading to the back of the house, closer to the cliffs. She was definitely a vampiress. Or, at least, that's what I'd call her.

Outside, the air felt thicker—as warm and humid as the miniature artificial rainforest inside Hank's lab back in Brooklyn. Someone was playing classical music on a piano. The yard was bright green; it squeaked when you stepped, and the blades of grass shined in the sunlight.

"Is this AstroTurf?" Ava asked.

Matt crouched and pressed his fingers to the fake grass. "Weird. She must have flown this in, too."

The edge of the cliff was only a hundred feet away, so it wasn't exactly the ideal spot for a game of catch. A poorly tossed football would send the receiver right over the edge.

157

We turned left, toward the music, and found a small group spread across the artificial lawn. One table was stacked four feet high with beautifully wrapped presents. Another was piled with desserts. There were only ten people at the party, and three of them were working, including two servers and a tuxedoed man with long gray hair who was playing the piano. Maya's uncle, David, huddled with Betsy, the dental hygienist who'd produced the nose vacuum. At the dessert table, Derek was subtly trying to sneak a few cream puffs. Clementine was sitting with her back against the wall of the house, wearing a flowered dress and playing on her phone. A few steps away, Steven was talking to his mother and the king, who stood with his back to the ocean, telling them a story. The bazillionaire was looking at everyone but him. Steven saw us but didn't react at all. Not a smile, not a sneer. Nothing. And I didn't see Maya, Ben, or our chief suspect.

I leaned closer to Ava. "Where are all his friends?"

"Maybe this is it," she said.

"Kildare's not here," Matt whispered.

Ava arched her eyebrows in the direction of the windows above us. "Maybe he's watching us," she suggested.

"Where's Hank?"

Matt checked his watch. "He said he and Rosa might be a few minutes late."

The vampiress held a tray of appetizers in front of the birthday boy. He stared down with shocked disapproval at the neatly stacked pile of cheese sticks. "Those are mine!" he said. "Those cheese sticks are my personal supply. You are not to just give them out to these"—he waved both his hands in the air—"people."

A booming laugh swung our attention back to the king. He was in hysterics, hands on his wide hips, eyes closed, roaring with joy at his own joke. Matt raised his eyebrows at something behind me. Hank and Rosa were hurrying around the corner. "Greetings!" Hank said. "Nice tie, Jack. Did we miss anything?"

Rosa plucked a small toasted sandwich off a passing waiter's tray, popped it into her mouth, and walked over to us carrying a tall, thin glass filled with a bright green liquid. She chewed, then tucked the appetizer into the side of her mouth like a squirrel storing food. "Sorry we're late," she said. "We were going over a few possible changes to the TOES."

Hank stared off into the distance. "I had this really, really interesting idea about energy generation and storage, too," he said. "How to build a better battery, you know?"

"That would be amazing," Matt said. "What are you thinking?"

Lifting his hands to his head, Hank moved them around as if he were shampooing his very short hair. "Still percolating," he said. "Not ready for discussion yet. Great potential, though. Great potential. One of your ideas inspired me, Jack."

His words faded into a mumble at the end. Did he say I inspired him? I clasped my hands in front of my chin and leaned forward. "I'm sorry, Hank, I think I misheard you, but did you say—"

But Hank's curious mind had already found its next target. He pointed to Rosa's drink. "What's that?" he asked.

159

She handed it to me, and for some reason, I took it. Rosa made a putrid face. "Pureed broccoli and lemon water. It's absolutely vile, but when I first got to Nihoa I told one of the kitchen staff I loved it, and now they keep bringing me them. No backsies."

Ava laughed. My new drink smelled like a cheap salad bar. "Thanks," I muttered.

Rosa pulled out a partially chewed pen and pointed it around the small crowd. "So which one of these folks sabotaged my prototype? The pianist?"

I pushed the pen out of the way. "Not so obvious!"

"Sorry, Detective," she replied.

"I don't know him," I admitted. "Has he been here the whole time?"

"He was flown in to perform," Hank said.

A gust of wind roared through the party, blowing a stack of napkins onto the grass. A short, tanned caterer with a crew cut rushed to collect them as the vampiress moved toward us with a tray of sizzling, bite-sized lamb chops. My brother tracked her like a hunter.

"Kind of sad, right? Four kids at his birthday party," Rosa said. "Makes you feel for Steven a little."

"A weird party's better than no party at all," Ava replied. "At least Ashley's trying."

"We did try!" Hank protested. "We had that surprise party for you."

"Yeah, and half the guests were robots."

"Excuse me for a second," Matt said, quick-stepping over to the lamb chops. He grabbed two in each hand, plus a few of the fallen cocktail napkins, before hurrying back. He looked like Wolverine, only with lamb chops instead of Adamantium claws.

"Hey, it's not my fault we barely know any normal kids," I added. "And you're the one who gives the robots names."

"They deserve them," Ava replied. "Besides, you had the surprise a week after my birthday."

"That is an odd way to surprise someone," Rosa noted. The miniature sandwich was still stuck in the corner of her mouth. How long was she going to keep it there?

Matt had already mauled his lamb chops. Now he stood with four stripped bones, some greasy napkins, and no garbage can in sight. Subtly I pointed to his jacket pocket. He wrapped up the bones, wiped his hands, and shoved them inside. Then he picked a piece of meat from between his teeth with his pinky nail.

The pianist finished his tune. Ashley and a few others clapped. The king shoved two fingers into his mouth and whistled. Seated against the wall, focused on her phone,

Clementine held up one hand and snapped her fingers in appreciation.

Rosa stood close to Ava. "That Clementine girl is an odd little particle."

"Those are the most interesting kind," Ava replied.

Now Rosa pointed her pen at me. "Is she on your list of suspects, Jack? You never know with the quiet ones."

Before I could answer, my sister put her hand on my shoulder and winked at Rosa. "I'll go do a little research," she offered.

Hank whispered, "She likes you, Rosa."

He was right. I glanced at Matt. Since when did Ava wink at other people? I was considering butting into my sister's conversation with Clementine, but then Maya walked out of the main house and I froze like a busted smartphone.

Normally, Matt's the awkward one at parties. When *The Lonely Orphans* was published, I practically had to remote-control him through the book signings and events. Turn this way, I'd say. Talk to him. Nod to her. No instruction was too small or insignificant. At one book reading I had to remind him to go to the bathroom. But now, seeing Maya, I was the socially frozen one. Moving was impossible. I felt like someone had poured cement into my kicks. My legs were wobbly, and I noticed that I was aggressively tapping the fingers of my right hand against my leg. I stopped. Then I rocked from side to side.

A muffled British voice said, "Keep going!"

Now this was really freaking me out. Hank and Rosa had sauntered off in search of better appetizers, but my brother was still standing next to me. "Did you hear that?" I asked. "The woman's voice?"

Matt stared down at my high-tops. "Your shoes," he said.

Since when was he interested in style? "I was going to wear nicer ones, but Ava said—"

"No, Jack, the voice is coming from your shoes. You got those at the lab, right?" I nodded. "They're weight-loss sneakers. They count your steps and encourage you to move instead of sitting on your butt. There are little speakers near the ankles."

Normally, I would have thanked him for proving that I wasn't losing my mind. But then Maya smiled at me across the fake lawn, and I completely forgot what we were talking about.

The caterer with the crew cut passed by again, now with a tray of what looked like ginger ales. Matt held one in front of me. "Drink this," he said.

The rush of bubbles and sugar helped me bounce back. So did the powerful taste of peanuts. I spat out a shower of the soda.

"Nutty, isn't it?"

Steven was approaching with his typical scowl, and a glass of the strange soda in hand.

163

"Happy birthday," Matt said.

"Whatever," Steven answered.

Behind him, back against the wall, I noticed Ava and Clementine whispering to each other and laughing. I'm not sure I'd ever seen Ava make a friend that quickly. Steven pointed to them. "Oh, look, they're friends," he said sarcastically. "How cute."

How do you respond to a comment like that? You change the subject. "So, Steven, you're thirteen?" I asked.

He ignored me. "Did you hear Marek, the pianist?" he asked Matt. "Supposedly he was a child prodigy, like us, but then he grew up and, well, you heard. That song was almost entirely off tempo."

I held up my glass. "Is this peanut butter soda?"

"Indeed," Steven said. "A delicacy in some parts of the world." He pointed to the gift table. "Presents can be left over there." Then, with surprising quickness, he reached out and flicked one side of my bow tie. "Look at you. All dressed up. How . . . special."

The number of times I've desperately wanted to know kung fu is pretty small. A kid stole my iPod on the subway platform once, then dared me to try to get it back. A swift kick to the legs would have been helpful there. In first grade, I was pelted by multiple meatballs during a cafeteria food fight. Dodging a few of those sauce-covered bombs would have been nice. Another time, a crooked Australian had tried to pull me down into a partially frozen sea at the South Pole. A little kung fu would have been great then, too. But standing there in front of Steven after he'd flicked my bow tie, I desperately wished I'd been able to stop his hand in midair. With my mind? Sure, that would've been ideal, but my fist would have been fine, too. Or maybe even just my index finger. No: my pinky finger. Then, with my little finger blocking his hand, I could've said something cool like, *Special? You want to see special?*

But way more awesome.

The sliding glass door opened, and I noticed Steven staring at the woman who stepped through—the wild-haired one I'd seen once before. She hurried to the gift table, carefully stacked a present, then grabbed a pair of lamb chops. Steven watched her furiously the whole time, and she glanced at him before rushing back inside.

"What was that all about?" I asked.

"Nothing," he snapped. "That was no one." He opened his eyes wide and clapped. "Anyway! I'd thank you for coming, but the pleasure is all yours. So eat, drink, enjoy yourselves. The fun is just beginning."

Was the party fun? That depends on your standards, I guess. Ava definitely liked it when we all went inside and Skyped with a famous software developer about programming. She sat next to Clementine, and when the guy started showing off coding tricks, they both grabbed napkins and jotted down notes. The trivia showdown was a hit, too. Matt almost didn't play—Hank caught him sneaking away to study for his test again just before the start. But then my brother got way into it; he and Ava and Steven were tied going into the last round. The birthday boy won, but only because Hank shot my siblings a death stare before the final question. He might as well have yelled, "Get it wrong!" And they did, and Steven did this weird little celebratory dance that reminded me of a kitten chasing its own tail. If I still had my phone, I would've posted it to YouTube. It wouldn't have gotten as many views as my fake puppy CPR video, but there was definitely some potential.

166

Otherwise, the party was kind of a dud. I was hoping for a pineapple-tossing contest. Or a potato-sack race. Maybe one of those games where you roll people up in toilet paper. Would a little obstacle course have been so hard to arrange?

There were rumors of a fireworks show later that night, but I was doubtful.

Even my detective work was boring. I poked around the first floor when no one was looking, hoping I might find Kildare. There was a box packed with fireworks sitting outside Ashley's office, but Harriet rolled up behind me when I went to check out one of the roman candles. Startled, I hurried back outside. Kildare had finally shown up. He was standing against the wall, checking his phone. The pack with the two swim fins was on the ground next to him. I walked over. "Do you always have that with you?"

"Yes."

"Why?"

"So I'm ready."

"For what?" I asked.

"Anything," he said.

"What's in there?"

"Everything you'd need to survive."

"Survive what?" I asked.

"Anything," he snapped. "Where's the cat?"

For a moment I had no idea what he was talking about. "Oh, right, Mr. Winkles," I said. I pulled the charm out of my pocket.

"Good," Kildare said. "Now go away." He flicked his fingers back toward the rest of the group.

At sunset, Ashley called everyone over to the center of the fake grass as the HR-5 rolled out of the house. All the guests gathered around her and Steven; Kildare was the only one who remained in place. "I hope you're all enjoying yourself. There will be plenty more activities, including a fireworks show that will rival the best in the world." I looked to Matt, Ava, and Hank with excitement. None of them were quite as thrilled. But Betsy, the dental hygienist, was clapping. "Before we get to all that, though, my son has something to show us. As you know, artificial intelligence is one of the great challenges of our time, and I'm not talking about the kind that wins chess matches or guides self-driving cars," she said with a nod to Hank. "I'm talking about true artificial intelligence, the kind that would allow a robot to talk to a person in such a rich, deep manner that this conversation would be no different than one between two normal people. My brilliant son," she said after a pause, "is remarkably close to solving this problem."

The sliding glass door opened again. The wild-haired young woman took one step onto the turf, noticed the robot, and froze. The birthday boy's face turned white. He lifted his hand to his mother's shoulder. She shivered and took a half step away. "Sorry, Ashley, but if you could just wait one—"

"Don't be modest, dear. You're ready. You told me so yourself."

The woman had left the sliding door open in her rush to return inside. I heard her trip on the stairs. Seconds later, a door slammed.

"Yes, but I just need a few minutes to tune up the machine." He walked slowly around the robot, like he was inspecting a car for dents.

"We could do the fireworks first," I suggested.

No one answered. Ava was whispering to Hank, "What's he talking about, 'tuning up' Harriet? What's he doing?"

"I'm not sure," Hank said.

Smiling wide, Ashley addressed the rest of us, "This will just take a minute!"

Suddenly the robot spoke. "Good evening, Mr. Hawking."

Seriously? He had his robot call him "Mr. Hawking"?

The birthday boy blinked, gulped, and approached the humanoid. "Good evening, HR-5."

Ashley was silently clapping in approval already. Ava whispered to Matt that greetings weren't at all hard to program.

"Experiment number forty-six," Steven said. "Ready?"

"Experiment begun," the robot replied. "What would you like to talk about?"

Steven paused and leaned his head to the right. "It is feeling a little cold tonight," he said.

"Indeed," the robot replied. "There is a low-pressure system approaching from the south. Today's high temperature was eighty-nine degrees Fahrenheit, and clear, but severe weather events are probable for the next few days."

"Ask it if we'll still need the air-conditioning!" the king shouted with a laugh.

After a brief pause, the robot began, "Air-conditioning

169

is a modern convenience designed to cool a room below the ambient temperature."

Steven glared at the king. "Are you done? Good. Now, HR-5, do you think it will be safe to fly tomorrow?"

"That depends on the skill of the pilot," the robot replied.

"Wonderful!" Hank declared with a laugh. Then he leaned over to Ava. "Programming a sense of humor is a tremendous feat."

"That was funny?" I whispered to Matt. But he didn't hear me. My brother and sister both were observing the robot and its long-haired, thirteen-year-old handler with a combination of shock and skepticism. Ava was squinting, her mouth hanging open ever so slightly, and Matt's focused, half-closed eyes suggested he was trying to find a flaw. My siblings just didn't want to believe Steven Hawking was this smart.

After a few more exchanges about the weather and the food, Steven informed the HR-5 that the experiment was over. Ashley clapped. The king went to lift Steven up on his shoulders, but the birthday boy dodged the attempt and hid behind his mother. Clementine snapped her fingers in appreciation. The islanders, after a glare from Ashley, applauded. I heard Derek asking if the robot could clean teeth.

"Maybe it was a Mechanical Turk," Matt muttered to Ava.

BILL NYE AND GREGORY MONE

"What's that?" I whispered.

"It's when someone speaks through the robot," Ava answered. "So you think the robot's really intelligent, and that you're talking to a machine, but you're actually conversing with a person."

"Kind of like the Wizard of Oz?" I suggested.

Neither of them answered. "Sort of, yes, Jack," Hank said. "But I would hesitate to accuse our friend of deception, kids. Jealousy dulls sharp minds."

While my siblings huddled to pick apart what they'd just seen, I resumed studying Kildare. Never too closely. Only in a subtle way. Like a spy, really, so that no one would notice. Especially not Kildare himself.

Then someone behind me whispered, "Why do you keep staring at him?"

I shivered. Maya. "I wasn't staring."

"No?"

"No." She glanced at my bow tie and smiled ever so slightly. Was that a good thing? Or was the smile really a smirk? "I'm just observing."

"There's something suspicious about him, definitely," she said. Was she mocking me? No. Or at least I didn't think so. "After you grilled my grandfather, I looked you all up," she continued. "That was quite a story about the South Pole. But we're not that kind of crazy."

172

I blushed, then stammered, "I . . . I didn't mean to—"

"No, no, it's okay," she said. "I get it. You're just trying to figure out what happened. So what do you think now?" she asked. "You're thinking it might be the SEAL?"

This probably wasn't my greatest moment as an investigator, but I told her everything. And of course I did it without realizing that Ava was standing behind me, listening.

"Secret's safe with you, eh, Jack?"

"I—"

"Sorry we thought it was you guys," Ava said.

"No worries. It makes sense. We'd be the obvious choice. But I think—" Maya's grandfather crossed the fake lawn with a ukulele under his arm. "Oh, no."

"What?" I asked. "You're not leaving, are you?"

"No, the opposite. If they start playing, we could be here for hours."

Ben invited her to join them, but she declined. Then he pointed his instrument at the king and asked her quietly, "Does he look familiar to you? I recognize him from somewhere."

"The TV ads," she said. "Not to mention the billboards."

"No, it's something else," Ben said, walking away.

By ten o'clock, the party was slowing, and we still hadn't seen the supposedly world-class fireworks display. Steven had practically screamed at the vampiress and the other

173

caterers to find his firecrackers, but they couldn't find the box. Unfortunately, besides the birthday boy, I was the only one who seemed to care.

The islanders were still strumming their instruments. Hank, Rosa, and the gray-haired pianist were sitting with them in a circle on the artificial turf, and our mentor was singing along, guessing the words to the songs as he went. Kildare remained at the wall, like a statue with a smartphone. At one point, I went to check if he was sleeping, but he barked at me to go away before I even got close. Clementine and the king had gone back to their rooms, and the Hawkings had disappeared after giving up their search for the fireworks.

Nothing nefarious was happening. Or not that night, anyway.

Matt talked us into moving to the roof so he could test out his new telescope, and under the bright stars, he and Maya started arguing about the constellations. She had different names for almost every star and planet, and they were talking about Mars when I noticed someone moving down the hill. I grabbed the telescope and swung it toward the path.

"Hey, what are you—"

"Shh!" I said. "Look."

"What is it?" Matt asked.

Ava pressed her eye to the lens. "Who is that? What's he doing?"

After Matt and Maya took turns at the telescope, I looked again through the lens. The path was dark and the figure was moving quickly. I adjusted the focus. Two long diving fins were sticking out the top of his backpack, and the small, stocky man pounced down the hill toward the beach with the sure, light steps of an accomplished badminton player.

12
THE BRUTAL
BREATH OF PAKA'A

HE WAS ALREADY OUT OF SIGHT WHEN WE BURST through the front door. We went to grab Hank, but he was still singing with the group. They'd moved on to rock-and-roll-style songs, and Hank was wailing about how they were born to run or something like

that. There was no way we'd be able to extract him without all the others noticing. "Let's just go," Matt suggested.

I convinced everyone to leave their phones in the house so Kildare wouldn't see us coming on his tracking app. As we rushed down the path, Matt said I sounded like an elephant. But he didn't exactly run like a gazelle, either. The girls, on the other hand, were annoyingly fast and almost silent. Was the Greek god of running a girl? Or was that the Roman one?

By the time the path cut through the rocks and curved down to the beach, I was breathing heavily. I yanked off my bow tie and shoved it into my back pocket with the notebook. My feet were sweating and my high-tops were talking again. "Keep going," the British lady said. "You're doing great!"

I agreed.

In the lead, Ava stopped with one foot forward and held out her arms.

"What?" Maya whispered.

"Thought I heard something."

"Don't stop now," my sneakers said.

"What was that?" Maya asked.

"Long story," Matt said. He pointed to the almost empty beach. "*Vader* and *Luthor* are both gone." The only boat on shore was Maya's handmade craft.

I could see the white spray of a powerboat's wake far out in the water. "There he is."

"What now?" Ava asked.

"We follow him," Maya said.

"In what?" I asked.

She pointed to her boat. The boat she hadn't finished yet.

The boat she'd named after a coconut.

"It's almost a mile," Ava said. "Paddling out there will take us forever. If you had an engine, then maybe . . . what?"

Maya winced and shrugged. "It kind of has an engine."

"What do you mean, 'kind of'?" I asked.

"I hate admitting this, but my grandfather let me cheat a little," she explained. "There's a small outboard on the stern. That's why we took this to shore tonight instead. Once I finish the sails and rigging, I'll get rid of the engine, but for now it's a safety measure."

"Let's do it," Matt said.

The boat had been pulled up onto the sand bow first, out of reach of the water, and the outboard engine was wrapped in some kind of cloth, hidden from view. My brother pushed at the bow but the boat didn't budge. For three strong adults and a wrinkled but fit grandfather, moving the boat probably wasn't even that hard. Now it was up to three scrawny kids and a brawny geek with his head in the stars. All three of us looked to Maya for instructions. She didn't offer any. "My uncle made it look easy," she said. "You just kind of lift and push."

"He's built like a wrestler," I noted.

Matt stood between the two wooden hulls, at the edge of the platform in the middle of the boat. "Is this strong enough to push against?"

"It should be," Maya said.

"Your confidence isn't exactly overwhelming," Ava said.

"Would you rather I lied?"

"I'll push from here," Matt said, "and then the rest of you push from the sides, closer to the water."

I took one side, Ava and Maya the other. Matt counted to three, and we started. My feet dug down into the sand. My fingers ached. Matt grunted, which seemed a little unnecessary. Then he let go and shook out his hands. "It's not moving," he said. "Gravity is a stubborn force."

"No, it's not just gravity," Ava said. "This is a friction problem, too."

In the two years since I'd lived with those two, I'd learned to shorten my requests for explanations to a simple word. "Translate," I said.

"It's not just the weight of *Niu*," Ava explained. She scooped up a handful of sand and poured it out slowly. "If we were on a slick surface—"

"Like a pan coated with butter?" Maya asked.

"Or a buttered living room floor," I added.

Maya squinted at me. "Why would anyone butter a living room floor?"

That little thought gem had slipped out a little too quickly. My brain/mouth gate was failing again.

Ava bailed me out. "Forget the butter," she said. "The point is, gravity is holding it down, and all this sand is holding it back."

So were we supposed to butter the bottom of the twin hulls?

"If we lift it a little more, though . . ."

Matt picked up her thought like a runner grabbing a relay baton. "Then we might be able to overcome both and get it moving . . ."

"And then once we get a little momentum . . ." Ava continued.

"The momentum will overcome the other forces," Matt finished.

A few seconds of silence followed. Did Maya understand what they were talking about? For her sake, and maybe mine, I asked, "And then?"

Matt slid his right hand forward, palm down, onto his left hand. "And then we hit the water."

"So," Maya said, "basically, we just lift and push?"

"Right," Ava said with a shrug. "Lift and push."

They could've just said that to begin with. Maya hurried over to my side. At first I was thrilled. Then I realized this meant she thought I needed help more than Ava. "I'm fine," I said. "Go back to Ava's side."

"I'm fine, too," Ava called across.

Maya shrugged and moved to the back with Matt. "Ready, set, go!" he said.

I dug my feet into the sand and lifted. Did I lift my side higher than Ava hoisted hers? Probably. I don't know for certain, and I wouldn't have wanted an official measurement, but I had a good feeling. *Niu* lurched forward, then slid so fast that Matt lost his balance and fell into the sand. The boat stopped. Maya laughed slightly, through her nose.

"We had it!" Ava said.

"One more," Matt said.

Niu slid again. Holding the hull up on one side and racing down the sand wasn't easy. I stumbled. The boat dropped to my side, but the very back of the stern splashed down against the edge of the water. Matt kept pushing, driving *Niu* farther. Maya and Ava joined him at the back and with a final, powerful effort, thrust the boat into the water. My siblings jumped on immediately, and the boat rocked from side to side while Maya stood in waist-deep water, holding a wooden cleat at the bow. "You joining us?"

Brushing the wet sand off my button-down shirt, I splashed ahead into the water, and a strange kind of shock jolted through my feet and up to my knees.

"The electronics in those sneakers aren't totally water-proofed," Ava said.

Yeah. I knew that. "I was testing them," I lied.

Maya was watching the surface closely. I pulled myself up out of the water, onto the platform. "What do you see? Sharks?"

She pushed the boat until she was standing in stomach-deep water, then climbed up and hurried to the platform as we drifted away from shore. She nodded to the water off to our right. Then she held her free hand out flat and moved it from side to side. "See the little ripples on the surface? They appear and vanish in seconds." Now she pointed to my left. "Again, right there!" In the moonlight, tiny waves rushed across the surface, then disappeared like ghosts. "We call it the breath of Paka'a, the god of wind."

"It's just wind," Matt said. "There's no god behind it. Just friction again, only instead of the boat scraping against the sand, it's the air rubbing on the water."

Maya moved to the stern. She unwrapped the engine and lowered it into the water. "It's not just a breeze. Paka'a's breath is a particular kind of breeze. The first whispers of a powerful wind—the signs of a coming storm."

All their talk of wind reminded me of Ashley's airborne odor blasts in the submarine. Was there a Hawaiian name for that noxious gas? Or a god of foul odors? If so, the bazillionaire needed to make him an offering.

"The storm Harriet mentioned?" Ava asked. "That's supposed to hit tomorrow, right?"

"Yeah, but it looks like it's coming early." Maya sighed, pointing to the south.

Far out on the horizon, the sky was black, but overhead, the air was clear, the stars as bright as distant spotlights.

The engine sputtered, then started. A puff of black smoke

billowed out. "We found it at the dump," Maya admitted. "But it's been pretty reliable."

The boat swung around and headed toward the lab. If someone had suggested we turn back, I wouldn't have protested. The farther we cruised away from shore, the more I wondered whether this was worth the effort. We could've waited for Hank. We could've hung around on shore, then confronted Kildare when he returned. But now we'd committed, and no one had the courage to be a coward.

The breeze was blowing one minute, gone the next, but the puffs of wind were getting stronger and stronger. For a second I thought old Paka'a might be real. Every shadow and swirl on the water made me think of sharks, but I didn't actually see one. Still, it would have been nice to know for certain. "Does someone want to check that shark-tracking app on their phone?" I asked.

"You convinced us to leave our phones at the house," Matt reminded me.

Right. Yeah. That seemed like a great idea at the time.

Matt leaned over the side and ran his hand along the wooden hull. "This is really amazing," he said to Maya. "I can't believe you built this yourself."

"It has taken me almost a year," Maya said. "My parents think it's crazy. But they're always too busy to interfere much, you know?" We didn't. "They're just not water types,

183

either. They think my grandfather and my uncle are insane, but they're always working, so every day after school and weekends, I've been building *Niu*. Sometimes I wish I just played sports like everyone else. Maybe join the surf team, you know? Or badminton. That's an incredible game." I glanced at Ava. Who knew badminton was so popular? "But my grandfather says I'll have plenty of time to be a kid when I grow up."

My brain froze. What was that supposed to mean?

"I still think it would be better with a bigger, cleaner motor and a nice GPS navigation system," Ava said.

"What do you have to do to finish?" I leaned over the side. "I mean, it floats, right? No holes or anything?"

"A few little items. The sails are almost ready, but I don't have the lines to raise or work them."

"That shouldn't be hard."

"I have to make the lines myself, the traditional Polynesian way."

"Are you serious?" Ava asked, nearly shouting. "Out of what?"

"Palm fronds and hemp, from the flax plant. Maybe it's a little extreme," Maya admitted, "but there's something really cool about the whole process, too. Most people use all this technology today and have no idea how it works or how it's made."

184

"I do," Ava said.

"Yeah, you're different. And this isn't just about how things work, either. It's history. My history. Don't you ever want to get in touch with your own heritage? Your customs?"

"I don't know them," Ava snapped. "I don't know where I'm from."

"Oh, I—"

"Shh!" I said. Maybe that was a little rude of me. They were having a serious conversation. Absolutely. But Ava hated that subject. She looked like she wanted to jump off the boat and swim back to our apartment on the other side of the world. And I couldn't tell whether Maya felt terrible or if she was still burning from Ava's question about the lines. Either way, we were only a boat's length from the dock, and we were trying to sneak up on a Navy SEAL. This was probably a good time to be quiet. "Cut the engine," I said.

Both *Vader* and *Luthor* were tied to the dock.

Once we were close enough, Ava sprang off the boat. A rope lay coiled like a snake on the deck. She tossed one end to Maya, who wrapped it around a cleat on the left side of *Niu*. Matt and I jumped off, and she followed. Then Ava hurried to the door. "Who knows the code?" she asked.

So apparently the door was locked. And there was a code. "Not me," I said.

"What now?" Maya asked.

185

The wind was blowing harder behind us. My siblings were looking to me for an answer. Their brains weren't tuned to this particular frequency. But mine wasn't either. Minor mischief? Sure. But picking a lock wasn't quite in my skill set. I tried the handle, just in case. Then I smelled something unexpected. "Is that smoke?" I asked.

Maya was pointing to my feet. Thin clouds were drifting out below the door. I heard distant popping noises. A bright yellow light flashed through the gap. Then purple and red bursts followed. "Are those—"

"Fireworks?" Matt said, finishing my sentence.

The lights flashed faster now. It sounded like someone had ignited an entire crate full of roman candles.

Ava backed away. "Indoor fireworks? That's not a very bright idea. You could set the place on fire."

I'm not sure she realized what she'd said. "That's what he's doing!" I shouted. "He must have stolen all the fireworks for Steven's party. Now he's trying to set the whole place on fire!"

Maya was already untying *Niu*. "We have to get out of here."

"Shouldn't we take something faster?" I suggested.

Matt jumped into *Vader*, stood at the wheel for an instant, then hopped back onto the dock and climbed into *Luthor*. "No keys in either of them," he said.

The wind was clawing at the water. If Paka'a was real, he was losing his temper. The dock shook, then rolled to one side, dipping into the ocean before recoiling. Water washed over the dock and down into the stairs. The smoke stopped briefly, then poured out from under the door. Ava was already on *Niu* with Maya. "Get on!" she cried.

Matt and I planted our feet on the dock, pushed *Niu*, and jumped aboard. The boat drifted. Maya was cranking the outboard engine, but it wouldn't start.

"What about the paddles?" Matt yelled.

Maya didn't answer. She was yanking on the pull cord to start the motor, but it wasn't even sputtering. "It's dead," she said.

Ava hurried to the stern and inspected the side. "No gas. Do you have a spare tank somewhere?"

Maya shook her head.

"Where are the paddles?" Matt asked again.

"I don't know, okay?" Maya said, her voice filled with frustration. "They must have fallen off when the dock rocked up and down."

"Then how are we supposed to get back to shore?"

Ava stared at the island. "We have to swim."

Had my sister lost her mind? The shore was almost a mile away. And there were sharks in the water. "I'm not swimming anywhere," I said.

187

"Not to shore, Jack," Ava said. "Back to the dock."

The distance between our boat and the dock was growing fast. If we were going to get back there, we'd have to go now. But there were too many dangers—the waves, the current, the sharks. And the dock itself didn't look any safer than our floating history project. Smoke was still flooding out of the lab. The door blew off its hinges. Flames burst out in a violent rush, as if an angry dragon was charging up the steps.

"Scratch that plan," Ava said. "We're paddling for shore."

"With what?" Matt asked.

Ava leaned over the right side and dug in with her hand. I followed her lead. But our efforts were useless. The current was sweeping us in the opposite direction, past the lab and out to the open ocean. Maya shouted, then pulled her hand out of the water and sat back against the mast. The current was like a conveyer belt carrying us farther away by the second. The spray was splashing my face. The wind was ripping against the furled-up sails. The waves were crashing against the sides of *Niu*. My hands were already aching from gripping the wooden hand rails along the outside of the platform. And I was pretty sure that the two triangular fins sticking up out of the water twenty feet away did not belong to friendly dolphins. We needed help. And we needed it fast.

"We need to call Hank!" I shouted.

189

All three of them glared at me.

Oh, right.

"The boat—can she handle this storm?" Matt asked.

The roaring wind drowned out Maya's answer.

"Wait, did you say you think so?" Ava yelled.

Maya reached back and wrapped her arm around one of the low guard rails. "We're going to find out."

13
SPIDER SAILING

THE WEATHER INTENSIFIED QUICKLY. ALL NIGHT long we were slammed and battered and pelted by raindrops as hard as pebbles. The wind was cold enough to freeze a mug of hot chocolate. My hands were stinging and cramped from grabbing the railings, and I was clenching my teeth tight enough to crack them. Although no one said much, we kept looking up every few minutes to make sure we were all still there. A few times, Matt reached over and squeezed my ankle.

After what felt like a month, the wind slowed, and Maya insisted that the storm was passing. Early the next morning, as the sky was starting to glow, I tucked myself underneath the furled-up sails and managed to fall asleep. When I woke, the wind had settled from a howl to a strong breeze. The others were talking about Kildare and his destruction of the lab. Matt was wondering aloud how he'd escaped, if at all. I was too tired to listen, too cold and wet to think. My socks and sneakers were soaked through, and my clothes were somewhere between drenched and damp. The notebook in my back pocket had transformed into a sodden collection of papery mush.

A weak yellow light was glowing through the fog, as if someone had dialed down the sun with a dimmer switch. The waves were big but steady. During the storm it had felt as if we were on a plastic boat getting knocked around inside a bathtub. Now the swells were smooth and predictable as they rolled below us.

I sat up, held my knees to my chest, and studied our homemade life raft. The deck was about as wide as my bedroom and bordered by low wooden rails. Matt and Ava sat at the corners nearest the bow. Maya and I were at the opposite end. I leaned back and stretched. A chair would have been nice. A cushion, maybe. How her ancestors spent weeks on boats like this one I could not figure out.

"You're awake," Matt said. He was green and pale.

"Where are we?" I asked.

"I might be able to tell you that if we hadn't left our phones back at the house," Matt pointed out.

Ava shook her head. "GPS would be pretty nice right now."

I yawned. "Seriously, though, any idea where we are?"

"We're lost," Maya said.

My stomach roared, and I realized I was hungrier than a professional wrestler. "Did anyone bring food?"

"A little. We might as well take stock," Maya answered. She crawled to the middle of the deck and opened a hatch the size of a desktop computer screen. I inched forward to look. Inside the small storage space, she'd stashed a random mix of supplies, and she removed them one by one and laid them on the deck. A knife. A tiny, sharp hook that she'd carved from a fish bone. Two bottles of water. A chocolate bar, a beach towel with the image of a palm tree, a container of Pringles, and a can of root beer.

"No radio hiding in there?" Ava asked.

"My ancestors didn't have that kind of technology," Maya said.

"But they ate potato chips and candy bars?"

And used motors, I was going to say. But Maya probably didn't want to be reminded of her out-of-gas engine.

"My grandfather must have stashed all this stuff in here. He tells everyone he's a super healthy vegan, but he's really a junk food addict."

"Any chance you brought that collapsible fishing rod, Matt?" I asked.

"Yeah," he said sarcastically, "right here in my . . . no."

Maya spread out our possessions. "Anyone have anything else?"

I held on to my ruined notebook; I didn't feel like explaining it. The bow tie didn't seem all that useful, either.

But Matt had no problem emptying his pockets. He removed a clump of brown, greasy napkins from his pocket. He laid the mess down on the deck, unrolled the napkins, and revealed the four small lamb chops stripped of their meat. Yellowish clumps of gristle were still stuck to the bones. "Fat?" he asked. He looked ready to vomit.

I shook my head. He went to toss them overboard, but Maya stopped him. "We might actually want that at some point." Then she passed Matt and Ava each a bottle.

Ava sipped, then tossed me the water. "How in the world did you sleep?" she asked. "What's wrong with you?"

Maya pointed to the bottle. "Only a little."

"I'm thirsty," I said.

"So are we, but we don't know how long we'll be out here," Maya replied. She pointed to a funnel-shaped contraption with a wood frame and cloth sides near the bow. "There's a water collection system, but we don't know if it's going to rain again, so right now all we have are these two bottles and the water we gathered last night in the storm."

"Which isn't much," Matt said, answering my question before I had a chance to ask. "So, sip. Don't gulp."

After a painfully small drink I handed the bottle back to Ava. Now, about that nap. Was I really supposed to be embarrassed? The ability to sleep through a life-threatening situation should be considered a skill. A talent, even.

I stared out into the fog. "The storm's over?"

"For now," Maya said. "But remember what the robot said? The weather could be rough for a few days."

The horizon was empty in all directions. I thought back to the night before—Kildare's disappearance, the fireworks, the door blowing right off its hinges. There was no way the lab had survived. The TOES had to be completely ruined.

"Forget all that for now," Ava said when I brought up the subject. "We need to focus on finding land."

"Do you know which way we drifted?" Matt asked.

"Southwest, maybe?" Maya suggested. "I'm not sure."

Ava pressed her hands to the sides of her head, yanking her hair back. My sister never panicked. But some kind of storm was raging in that head of hers. She needed something to do. Fidgeting with gadgets normally helped her, but I didn't want to bring up the motor again.

195

Matt stood up and patted the furled-up sail that had been my bed. "What about these?"

Maya shook her head. "We don't have any line to string them up. I haven't finished that part yet."

The sails were bound together by thick straps. "Could these help?"

"That's not exactly line, Jack," Matt said.

For a minute no one spoke. I stared down at my shoes, and an alarm rang in my brain when I noticed the laces. Hurriedly I started pulling one out. "What about these?"

My brother sighed. "Maybe if you had something a hundred times that long. But that's a shoelace, Jack. That wouldn't even be enough for a toy sailboat."

Sometimes I wanted to put him in a toy sailboat.

Then Ava pointed at the laces with sudden excitement. "Wait, Jack, where did you get those? Were those always on your sneakers?"

"No, the originals were white. I swapped them out for this pair. I liked the color. Why?"

"Did you get the laces in the lab?"

I nodded. "On the Clutterbuck table," I added.

"Your friend Hank's lab?" Maya asked.

"Yeah." What was that little sign attached to them? The one I ripped off. I searched my brain. Luckily, this time I didn't get lost inside. "They're called spider laces or something."

"You're a genius!" Ava shouted.

"I am?"

"Well, no, not really," Matt added, "but you're awesome."

Gee. Thanks. I guess?

Ava crawled over to me, reached out, and grabbed one end of the laces. They stretched. I looked up, then hurriedly freed the lace from the last few holes. She held the bright yellow fabric up to the dull sunlight, turning it slowly in her fingers. One corner of her mouth moved out slightly—she wasn't ready to smile, not yet. She wrapped one end of the lace around her fist and handed me the other end. I followed her lead. Then we pulled in opposite directions. The lace stretched farther. There was a silvery color to the material now, too. "What the—"

"Keep pulling," Matt said.

We moved our hands to the middle, wrapped the line around our fists again, and yanked.

"Are those rubber bands or something?" Maya asked.

We kept pulling at the laces until they held tight. I grabbed with both hands and tried to stretch them farther, but they'd finally reached their limit. They were as thin as thread now, maybe fifty feet long, and impossibly strong. I yanked on the line once more and it held tight, digging into my skin.

The salty smell of potato chips filled the air as Maya popped off the lid. "Anyone want to explain?" she requested.

"These shoelaces are woven from artificial spider silk," Ava said. "The material is as strong as a steel cable but as thin as sewing thread."

197

I held out my hand. Maya counted out three chips and passed them over, then gave three to the others as well. Ava wasn't interested, though. She wrapped the shoelace around her elbow and hand, forming a coil, then passed it to Maya. "This'll work as line, right? We can use it to raise the sails. I know it's thin. It's certainly not ideal, but . . ."

Maya didn't answer. Her face was glowing, and it wasn't from the oily saltiness of those miraculously thin chips.

Matt pointed to my other sneaker. "Give me that one."

My foot was as damp as a wet towel. The odor was going to be powerful, and when I pulled off that high-top, the surrounding air actually rippled a little. I slipped off the other one, too. And the socks. Matt winced and scrunched his huge nose. Luckily the breeze was blowing from the bow to the stern, and the Pringles scent still hung in the air, so Maya wouldn't catch any.

"Wow!" she said, pressing the back of her hand to her nose. "That's pungent, Jack."

So she had a sharp sense of smell, too. I pointed to the mast. "How can we help?"

She said she'd take care of everything herself, and she did. I don't know how much time passed. Not one of us was wearing a watch. But I'd guess she worked for at least three episodes of *Duck Detective*. Using her hand-carved hook, Maya threaded the sail with the line, then ran it down through the wooden rings that extended the length of the mast. Matt offered to let her stand on his shoulders to work near the top, but she declined, scurrying up the skinny wooden mast with ease. Then she shimmied back down with the line wrapped around her fist and started pulling the spider silk hand over hand. I went to go help her, but Ava stopped me. "This is her thing," she whispered.

"Is it going to work?" I asked.

The sail rose to the top of the mast. The light wind pushed against the brown canvas and the boom swung, knocking Matt right in the chest. "I'm fine!" he yelled, but he was already falling backward off the side of the boat.

He fell flat on his back with a huge splash. I dove forward and lay on my stomach with one arm in the water. He grabbed me at the elbow. The wide-eyed terror on his face switched quickly to anger. "Don't you dare—"

Laugh? At a time like that? Never. Or not too much, anyway.

He climbed up on his own.

Maya stood holding the huge paddle that served as the boat's rudder. The spider lace was tied and wrapped around a wooden pulley to her right. "Watch the boom," she said to Matt.

"Yeah. Thanks."

The sail snapped full of wind. The boat lurched forward. "We're moving," I said. "That's good, right?"

"Yeah, but where are we moving?" Ava asked.

Matt pointed into the glowing fog. "Hard to tell, but the light looks strongest there, so I'd say that's the sun," he said. "Which means we're heading . . ."

"Northeast," Ava answered.

"So we just head that way and we'll hit Ashley's island?" I asked.

"Nihoa," Maya corrected me. "It's not her island. And unfortunately, no, it's not that easy."

Sitting on the deck, leaning back against the railing, Matt explained. "If we want to find land, knowing our direction isn't enough. We need to know where we are now. Otherwise we could sail right past the island and into the open ocean."

"When the stars rise, I should be able to figure it out," Maya said.

"That's a long time to wait," Ava noted, "and we better hope the fog clears by then."

"Someone could find us, too, right?" I asked. Hank would never let us drift out into the open ocean. He'd do everything he could to help us. "Your grandfather, maybe? Or your uncle?"

"They'll try," she said. "Otherwise my parents will kill them. I'm sure Ashley will send out a search party, too."

200

"They're going to have to search hundreds of square miles with very little visibility," Matt said. "I'm going to miss my test. The professor's going to fail me."

No one bothered to point out that this should've been the least of his concerns. And Matt didn't mention that our phones would've helped. But I was sure that's what they were all thinking. This whole mess wasn't all my fault. But I had played a critical role. I stared out at the empty sea. "There's still a chance someone could track us down, though, right?"

After way too long, Matt answered, "Sure, Jack. There's a chance."

That was good enough for me.

14
ANSWERS IN THE STARS

SO I'VE BEEN HUNGRY BEFORE. ABSOLUTELY. AND I know millions of people die of starvation every year. Or at least I think it's millions. That's what my second foster mom used to say when she'd serve me three microwaved chicken nuggets for dinner and I'd ask for more and she'd try to convince me that I was lucky to have gotten the first trio. As the daylight faded, and we sailed in what I hoped was the right direction, I wasn't thinking about all those millions of starving people. We were down to eight paper-thin potato chips and half a candy bar, but we'd agreed not to eat any more of that just yet, so I was just about ready to chew the soggy, fake leather tongues of my high-tops.

"Are we getting close?" I asked.

"That's the hundredth time you've asked that, Jack."

"Sorry."

"Eighty-seventh," Ava corrected. "I counted."

"Well, for the eighty-seventh time, I can't guess where we are until the stars rise."

"I know, I know, I'm just . . ."

"We all are, Jack."

Hunger was a major concern, but we had minor ones, too. The lack of a toilet, for example. We agreed on a look-the-other-way approach to the problem, and the three people who weren't taking care of their personal business would hum loudly while the fourth person was in the middle of the process. Toilet paper? We had a knife and a blue blazer that no longer fit my brother. I'll leave it at that.

As the sun continued dropping, I started tapping the sole of my sneaker against the wooden deck. Matt was telling me to stop when the sneaker spoke. "Keep going," it said, in that horribly cheery voice. "You're doing great!"

"What's with those things?" Maya asked.

Matt explained. Then I looked over at my restless sister. I handed her my high-top. "I guess they are waterproof. Maybe you can figure out how they work?"

Immediately Ava started trying to peel off the sole to get to the electronics inside. Matt dug the chops out of the remains of his pocket. "Anyone ready for one of these yet?"

The girls hesitated, but I grabbed a lamb chop and immediately started gnawing away at the yellow bits of fat and gristle. And it was positively scrumptious. Even the cartilage was a delight. Ava stared at me like I was some kind of deranged caveman, then she laid my sneaker on the deck and grabbed a chop of her own. Maya followed. Soon we were all chewing away happily, taking small sips of water to wash down the fat. I turned and stared at our wake, the swirling water and the distant rolling waves. Something splashed far away.

The light was fading. An orange glow hung over the sea.

I spotted a second splash. Between chews I asked, "Anyone else see that?"

Ava scooted to the back. "Was that a fish?"

"I think so."

She held up the bone and the few remaining strings of fat clinging to it. "What if we try to catch one?" she asked.

"How?"

She grabbed the leftover spider shoelace. "We have line." She pointed her chop at Maya. "You have that hook, right?" Maya nodded. "Then all we need is bait."

"The gristle will work," Matt said. "But I ate mine." He held up his chop; the bone was so clean it looked like it had been bleached.

Maya tossed hers at Ava's feet. "Be my guest," she said, wincing. "After that nastiness I might be a real vegan."

"Don't we need a rod?" Matt asked.

"No!" I answered. My enthusiasm startled them, and

they looked at me like I had four noses. But I actually knew what I was talking about. Before we'd left on the trip, Hank had given me a short little book to read. He said it was the only novel he'd ever enjoyed. I forget the author's name, but it was a really simple tale about an old fisherman battling with a huge marlin. And the guy hooked the monster using only a handheld line. "No," I said again, "we don't need a rod. We just let the bait trail behind the boat, and if we hook something, we pull it in by hand."

Surprisingly, they listened to me. As the fog gradually cleared, and the sky transformed from that yellowish glow into deeper and deeper blues, we watched an unusually long shoelace with a handcarved hook and a chunk of lamb fat at one end drift behind *Niu*. Personally, I've never understood fishing. There's just way too much waiting involved and not enough reward. It's like playing a game on your iPad that takes hours to load. And then when you do finally start to play, you lose on the first level and wait for it to re-load again.

When Matt finally felt a tug at the other end of the line, we all practically leaped for joy. Someone yelled, "Sushi!" But my brother pulled in an empty hook. We'd been picked clean. And some crafty fish was enjoying his or her first taste of lamb.

"Well, that didn't work," Matt said.

205

"We have enough to bait three more hooks," Maya reminded him. "Let's try again."

This time I held the line, wrapping it a few times around my fist like the old man in the book. While we waited, Ava worked on my shoes. She pulled a long, thin wire out of my mangled high-top. I don't know what she was doing, but she seemed happy.

The fog had finally disappeared. Bright white stars were appearing all across the sky, and Matt and Maya were watching them closely. How her ancestors used that mess of little white lights to find their way across the ocean was beyond me. They all looked the same, like we were sailing below an enormous, domed black ceiling with little white Christmas lights poking through. Matt stood near the bow of the boat and held his arms out wide like a preacher. With his head back and his eyes on the sky, he turned slowly, moving his hands up and down as if he were a football player who just scored the winning touchdown in a stadium full of cheering fans. "This is it!" he said. "This is what it's all about!"

"What's he doing?" Maya asked in a whisper.

I bit the side of my lower lip and shook my head. "I honestly don't know. Matt?" I asked. "What's up?"

He crouched in front of me, then pointed back up at the sky. "This is astronomy, Jack! Not sitting in front of my computer, cramming for some test, studying diagrams and data on a web page."

"Your test," Ava said. "Wasn't that today?"

"Yes," Matt replied. "And you know what? I don't care."

"You don't?" I asked.

"No!" He paused for a second, as if he was double-checking the truth of his answer. "Really."

"But you've been studying for a week," Ava said.

"I know. I know. But the whole point is to learn, right? And this is the place to learn! No artificial lights. No computers. Just you and the sky." Matt caught me staring at him. He stood and motioned to the stars. "Drink it in, Jack. Amazing, aren't they?"

He was right. They were beautiful. Hank has gotten us out of the habit of using the word incredible. He used to flinch when one of us said it. But these stars . . . well, they were stunning. And they were everywhere, shining like the headlights of a billion distant spaceships cruising toward Earth. I leaned my head back and rolled it from left to right. The dark and starlit sky was gorgeous, intense, frightening, and strangely cold. Hank is always talking about how complex life-forms are so ridiculously rare. Humans especially. But out there under all those stars, I felt about as special as a toenail clipping.

Then Maya pointed to something off the bow. "There it is!"

"The island?" Ava asked.

"No, tana mun!"

Matt squinted. "Tana who?"

"The star," she said. She pointed straight ahead, to the horizon. "Or at least I think that's tana mun. She rises in the northeast and sets to the northwest. So if that's her"—she turned around, pointing to several other distant stars, talking to herself—"then we're in roughly the right place, and we're heading the right way."

The line was tightening around my hand. Maya had cut part of Matt's blazer into long strips to help tie down the sails. I grabbed one of the leftovers and wrapped it around my palm.

"Tana mun? That's Vega," Matt said. "The second-brightest star in the northern hemisphere. It's only twenty-five light-years away."

Ava's eyes aimed upward in thought. "That's more than a trillion miles," she noted. "A lot more."

"And it's not Vega, it's tana mun," Maya insisted.

"What's the difference?" I asked. "We say pineapple, the French say . . ." Unfortunately I forgot the French word for that particular fruit. I just knew it was funny.

Ava pitched in. "*Ananas*. It has an *s* at the end, but you don't pronounce it. Very French."

"Sure. My point is"—the line was really digging into my hand now, but the strip of blazer was helping—"the point is

208

that you're using two different names for the same star. What matters is whether that one is going to help us get back to Ni . . . oww!" I grabbed the spider lace with my other hand and pulled, trying to loosen its stranglehold on my hand.

"Jack!" Maya said, pointing out at the water.

A glimmering silver fish leaped out of the water. The creature was as large as my brother and as beautiful as a brand-new Ferrari. And this fish was utterly and completely hooked onto the end of our line. I bit my lip. What now? Did I actually have to pull this thing in? Too excited to cheer or even speak, the others crowded around me, and we took turns gathering in the line, hand over hand, slowly and steadily, as if any sudden movement might loosen the hook from the mouth of the magnificent fish. In the book, the old man's catch leaped several times, but ours wasn't quite so dramatic. The creature didn't jump again, so we didn't even see it until its silver back was shining in the black water right beneath our boat. Maya leaned over the edge, holding both hands above the water, waiting, waiting, then grabbed the fish and tossed it up onto the deck, where it slapped its tail and wriggled at our feet.

209

So maybe it wasn't an award-winning monstrosity. The fish was only about as long as my forearm, and a little thicker than one of my pencil-thin legs. But still.

Shocked, Matt stared down at the creature. "You caught a fish."

I still couldn't believe it. "I caught a fish?"

"No, you caught dinner," Maya said. Then she laid her hand carefully across the scales, slid her fingers back, wrapped them around its tail, picked up the creature, and quickly slammed it back down onto the deck.

The little swimmer would kick no more.

All three of us stared at Maya in amazement. "What?" she said. "You weren't planning on eating it alive, were you?"

Maya laid the fish flat on the wood and scraped off the scales on both sides with her blade. She cut a crescent shape at the base of the head, then held the blade at an angle, and sliced into the tail. Next she inserted the tip of the blade near the base of the crescent, close to the fish's head, and cut back. She repeated this along the bottom, then set the blade into the slice she'd made near the tail and, using the knife like a saw, carefully cut off the meat. I was so mesmerized I forgot to breathe. Finally, she peeled off a huge strip of the white flesh and sliced it into cubes.

Raw fish is not really my thing. Sometimes Hank will take us out to one of his favorite sushi places near the lab, and I'll go for the plain old cucumber and avocado roll. No sesame seeds. No fish. Just rice, veggies, and soy sauce. But my first bite of that fish was just about the most delicious morsel of food I'd ever tasted.

Better than a burger.

Better than pizza.

Even better than an ice cream sundae.

Maya diced up a few more bites. I downed four more, then lay back and stared at the star they'd been arguing about before. What had she called it? Tana something? I pointed. "So back to what you were saying before, Maya . . . that star tells you we're going the right way?"

I shivered a little as she took my wrist and pointed it to a different light in the sky. "That's her, tana mun," Maya explained. "And yes, I think we're going the right way."

Matt smiled but said nothing. Maya let go of my wrist. I breathed. "Good," I mumbled. "That's . . . good."

We sailed through the night, taking turns sleeping and steering. The next morning, the sun wasn't up long before it started burning the back of my neck. Luckily, the breeze hadn't disappeared with the clouds, so *Niu* cruised, and for a few hours we were able to huddle in the shade of the sail. We'd picked the fish clean, but we saved a few chunks from the head and stomach to use for bait, in case we needed to catch another one.

With a little nourishment in my stomach, my thoughts turned back to Kildare. Who had paid him to sabotage the project? Why? If he knew we were onto his plan, he wouldn't want anyone to find us. He'd send them in the wrong direction. And unless Maya really was following those stars the right way, or Hank tracked us down, we'd waste away out in the middle of the ocean.

By the afternoon, Ava had transformed both my high-tops into a tangle of wires and metal components. Matt was constantly scanning the horizon, looking for any sign of land. Maya was watching the water closely, just as she had two nights earlier. "There isn't another storm coming, is there?" I asked.

"Maybe," she said, "but right now I'm trying to read the swells."

Without looking up, Ava said, "You can't read waves."

"Sure you can. My ancestors didn't just use the stars. They also figured out where they were on the ocean based on the direction of different swells and currents and whether they'd been bent around an island."

"That actually worked?" Matt asked.

"Supposedly," Maya said, "but I haven't really learned how to do it."

"Hey, you did pretty well with those stars last night," Matt said. "Tana mun showed us the way."

"I hope you're right," she said.

The water swirled in our wake. I counted four different shades of blue mixed in with the white lines of foam, then noticed a bird with white wings and hilariously bright red feet flying toward us. "Maybe that guy can tell us," I joked.

Matt and Maya turned and squinted at the sky. Maya lifted her hand to her brow, suddenly excited. "What is it?" she asked. "Can you see?"

"It's a bird," I said.

"No, what kind?" Matt asked.

Geniuses. Why did they always have to name things?

"That's a red-footed booby!" he shouted.

I laughed. Ava looked up from my mangled sneaker and glared. I held up my hands like a caught criminal. "What? He said it first!"

Matt clapped, then held his hands together. "Boobies are a kind of seabird. Amazing divers. They pursue their prey underwater." He tapped his head and neck. "And they have these cool little air sacs in their heads that protect them when they slam into the water chasing fish. The sacs are kind of like air bags in a car, you know? They absorb the force of the collision with the water."

This was not the time for a science lesson. "That's great, but we can't fly, you know," I added.

"They live on Nihoa," he explained. "That was one of the birds we saw taking off the other day."

"The clumsy one with the colorful feet?" Ava asked.

213

"Exactly!"

I cut in. "So if we follow him—"

"Or her," Ava noted. "In nature, mothers are often the more effective hunters."

"Sure," I said. "If we follow the bird, we get back to the island?"

"Maybe," Maya said. "They don't only live on Nihoa. It could be coming from somewhere else."

The bird was soaring ahead and to our right. If we were heading for twelve noon on an old-fashioned clock, the bird was flying more toward the two. "She's not quite going the same way," I noted.

"Following the stars like this, without any instruments, we could easily be off by thirty or forty miles," Maya admitted.

Forty miles? Seriously? She should've mentioned that earlier. "Then we're following the bird."

"Agreed," Ava said.

Maya turned the paddle, and *Niu* veered right, tracking the slowly disappearing seabird. By early evening we'd caught and devoured another fish, chomped the last of the chocolate bar, and eaten our way down to the final four potato chips.

I was imagining stabbing my fork into a piece of salted, juicy steak when Maya sprang to her feet and pointed into the distance. "Look!" she exclaimed. A kind of shadow hung near the horizon. "That's Nihoa! We're actually going to make it, guys. We're actually going to make it!"

The four of us jumped to our feet and started hugging and high-fiving and cheering. After I embraced my brother and sister, I turned to Maya to do the same, but she kind of held up one hand, so I figured she was going for the high five, and then I did the same, but something went wrong. I'm not sure how it happened, exactly, but the heel of my hand kind of knocked her on the forehead. She might have laughed about it—at least, I hoped so—but she didn't have the chance. A terrifying cracking, splintering sound stopped our celebrations.

A gust of wind had burst out of the sky, and the mast was suddenly bending awkwardly, like a tall man preparing for an impossible round of limbo. The mast split and splintered. Three feet above the deck, just above the boom, the wood snapped in half. Matt dove out of the way as the mast and the carefully hand-woven sail plunked into the sea with a hope-shattering splash.

215

15
FRANK TO THE RESCUE

SO, YEAH, THAT WAS BAD. HEART-CRUSHING, REALLY. The sail floated in the water, part of it tied to the busted mast and part to the boom. My siblings might be brilliant, but the brightest minds in history wouldn't have been able to get our ship sailing again.

The good news? We were all starting to agree that Maya was probably right about the dark blotch of light on the horizon. That was our island. And for once, the current was actually working with us, carrying us closer.

Unfortunately, the sail dragging in the water wasn't helping. "We have to get rid of it," I said, pointing to the busted rigging.

Matt tried to start the engine again. I didn't even bother to hope, and the motor didn't make a noise. Ava was pulling at her ponytail, frantically trying to come up with something. "What if we—"

"No, Jack's right," Maya said, "we need to shed this weight."

She started to untie the sail from the boom, but Matt grabbed the knife and cut it free instead. *Niu's* pace quickened, but Maya stared in silence at the broken and torn remains as they drifted in our wake. I took her by the shoulders and turned her around, pointing to the island. Before long, the jagged tooth had risen up over the horizon. We were actually going to make it to land. And I was going to make it to a real bathroom soon, too. I was about to cheer when Matt pulled a Hank and started drumming his fingers on his chin. "We're going to miss," he said.

"But we're on track—"

"No, he's right," Maya said. She crouched, held her thumb far out in front of her, glanced behind us, then stared ahead. "The current is going to carry us too far west of the island. We're going to miss by a mile."

"More like two," Matt said.

"What would Hank do?" I asked.

"We need to find a way to signal them," Matt suggested.

Maya stared at the island. "How?"

Ava grabbed the can of root beer from the storage compartment. "The aluminum on the inside," she said. "What if we cut it open, turn it inside out, then reflect the sunlight toward the island? Maybe they'll . . ." She hadn't even finished her thought when the sky darkened and the sun disappeared behind a screen of thick gray clouds.

I told myself and the others that our situation could be worse. Maya wondered how, exactly, things could possibly be even more terrible. "Steven could be here," I offered.

"With his mom," Matt added with a laugh.

"Or a shark could be stalking us," Maya added.

Finally she was catching on. "Seriously! Right? That would be terrible!"

Maya was pointing to something in the water behind me. She breathed out long and deep, her shoulders sagging. "No, really, a shark is following us."

"This is fantastic!" Ava exclaimed.

I thought she was being sarcastic. Or that she'd lost her mind somewhere back in the storm. "It is?" I asked.

"Do we have any bait left?" she asked.

"We're not catching a shark," Matt said. "I don't even know if we'd be able to get it up on the deck here. And if we did, it would probably chew off one of Jack's feet."

I glared at him. Why one of my feet?

"No, no, no," Ava said. "We're not going to catch it. I just want to lure it closer so we can grab the tracking tag."

"And why do you want to grab the tracking tag?"

She opened the hatch and removed the mangled remains of my left high-top. "This isn't just a sneaker, remember?" Ava said. "I've been trying to figure out how it works."

"I thought you were just fiddling," I said.

Ava held up an index finger. "Fiddling with a purpose."

"So?"

"So these sneakers use a pressure sensor to count your steps." She smiled and held out her hands, as if we were all supposed to understand what that meant. And Matt actually did.

"They don't even have accelerometers?" he asked.

"No!" Ava said. "Insane, right?"

The idea was as strange to them as a pizza without cheese.

Eyebrows scrunched, Maya turned to me. I gave her a "don't ask" look. To my siblings, I added, "Keep going."

"Well, if we can wire the pressure sensor to the battery inside one of those tracking devices, then we can switch it on and off," Ava said. Then, to Matt, she added, "And if we can switch it on and off, then we can . . ."

"Morse code?" Matt asked.

Ava turned her palms up and shrugged. "Do you think it'll work?"

Thankfully, Maya was running at my mental pace—more of a slow, sweaty, exhausted jog than a sprint. "I don't get it," she said. "How is this shoe going to help you use Morse code?"

219

"Imagine you're looking at the shark-tracking app," Matt said. "Normally the little red dots that represent each shark are steady, right? They don't blink or flash."

I pictured the screen in the lab, and the view on Steven's phone when he showed me the tracker.

"Right," Maya said.

"So now if we hook the pressure sensor to the battery on the tracking device, then those little red dots are only going to show up on screen when we're pressing the sensor, and activating the tracking device. When we let go . . ."

Matt was looking at me, passing the conversational football. I just hoped I didn't drop it. Hesitantly I replied, "No red dot?"

Matt slapped me on the back. "Exactly!"

"If we do it right," Ava explained, "the red dot will blink in the pattern of an S-O-S message."

"And when they see an S-O-S message coming from this location," Matt said, staring ahead at the island, "they'll know exactly where we are."

"So now we just have to hope that someone is watching their shark tracker."

"And we have to hope that they understand Morse code, too."

Now I held up my index finger. "Plus this hypothetical rescuer needs to see it before Kildare." Everyone paused. Ava pursed her lips and exhaled. Suddenly this plan didn't feel so golden. I pointed to the water. "Then there's the small matter of grabbing the tracking device off the shark's fin."

"Is that Elizabeth?" Matt asked.

"No," Ava answered. "I think that's Frank."

Maya asked my question for me. "How do you even know that?"

Ava pointed to the beast's dorsal fin. "Rosa showed us a few of their identifying features. See the scar at the top? That's Frank."

This was a relief. There had been a girl named Elizabeth in one of my second-grade classes, and she was an absolute terror. Unusually tall and strong, with a pointy chin and curly hair topped with a purple bow, she'd snap your favorite pencil in one hand just to watch you whimper. I still had nightmares about her. In my dreams she was fifty feet tall and snapped pine trees in two with her bare hands.

A shark named Frank was slightly less intimidating.

Matt stood up and leaned his weight onto the boom. "The boom is still strong. So what we'll do is tie someone to the boom here, lure Frank closer with some bait, then swing that someone out over the water to reach down and grab the tracking device."

"Off the shark," Maya noted.

"Right. Off the shark."

221

As if he was listening, Frank bumped against the port side of the boat. I nearly leaped into Matt's arms.

"Don't sharks jump out of the water?" I asked.

"Not all the time," Matt said.

In our current universe of four people, I had the strong feeling that Maya and I were the only sane ones. "So who's going to volunteer for that role?" she asked.

Everyone turned quiet. Matt looked at me first. Then Ava. And, after a few seconds, Maya, too. Clearly my siblings were waiting for me to volunteer. I closed my eyes. When I was younger I figured no one could see me if I couldn't see them. I thought shutting out the world made me invisible. But it didn't work then and it didn't work now. Slowly I opened my eyes, and my siblings were still staring at me hopefully.

"Wait, Jack, aren't you petrified of sharks?" Maya asked.

Yes. Absolutely. Tremendously. "Well, I mean, petrified is kind of a strong word—"

"No worries, I'll do it," Maya offered.

Oh, great. No worries? How could she be so casual? We weren't talking about being scared of an imaginary monster in your basement. That was a prehistoric assassin circling our boat. She should have been petrified, too. But now I definitely had to volunteer. "No, no, I'll do it."

She stuck out her tongue, breathed out, and slapped me on the back. "Phew! I was hoping you'd say that."

Matt held his hands out to his sides, as if he were supporting an invisible inner tube, then squatted slightly. "It's just that I'm a little too heavy, you know?"

One eye half-closed, Ava stared up at the sky. "And I'm . . . well, it was my idea, so I get a pass, right?"

Ten minutes later, I was tied to the boom by strips of the handmade sail and what remained of Matt's dinner jacket. The plan was to swing the boom—and me—out over the water, then lure Frank closer to the boat with our last few scraps of bait. That way, I could reach down and grab the tracking device off his fin. Now, if someone had explained it to me in those terms, I probably wouldn't have raised my hand. In fact, as Matt pushed the boom, swinging it away from the deck, I was feeling way more like dinner than a twelve-year-old kid.

"Ready?" Matt whispered.

No. Absolutely not.

This whole plan was ludicrous. Insane. Ridiculous.

But they were depending on me. "I'm . . . r-r-ready."

My brother tossed a fish head into the water.

Frank circled closer, his scarred fin cutting through the water like a jagged knife. The fish head floated directly below me, the pink strips of flesh and red blood clinging to the yellowish bones.

"What's he doing?" Ava asked. "He's not going for it."

223

"Maybe he's not hungry," Maya suggested.

I liked that idea.

"Or maybe it's not enough," Matt replied. He tossed another scrap into the water with a splash. This time, Frank darted over and snapped at the bait. He was only an arm's length away from me. I could've patted him on the nose. His teeth were yellow, crooked, sharp. And there were so, so many of them.

Matt yelped. Any other time I would've laughed at him. The fin darted below me as Frank snapped at the tossed bait. But I was still holding my arms locked to my sides, as far away from that creature as possible. The canvas and blazer ties dug into my stomach and legs. Holding my breath, I reached down to grab the device and missed, slapping his fin. The skin was surprisingly rough, like sandpaper. My clothes were soaked and I was shivering, but not from the cold.

225

"This isn't going to work," Ava said.

"We've got to try something else," Maya agreed.

"No, let's try again," I said. "I can do it."

Matt threw every last scrap of the fish into the water near the boat. Frank swung wide, like a tanker, then cruised in slowly. Was he actually full now? Or just skeptical of this sudden meal?

"Left," I whispered, "a little left."

They moved the boom just as the huge creature swam

below me. The ties loosened as I reached down for his fin. Then the binding around my chest came completely undone. From the waist down I was still tied to the boom, but the rest of me dropped. My hands splashed into the water. The shark lashed back and forth. My right elbow slammed into Frank's rough-skinned back, just beside his fin. And I was dangling down like his next snack. The water was splashing and churning. His tail slammed the hull of *Niu*. The boat rocked, and the boom dropped closer to the water. I covered my head with my arms. If I was going to be the sushi now, I was hoping he'd start with a small test-bite first, and save my brain. I screamed. But so did everyone else. Then they swung me back toward the deck so fast that my arms and shoulders slammed against the side of the boat. Matt reached down and grabbed the back of my shirt, yanking me up onto the deck as Maya and Ava hurried to free me. I dropped with a thud, and then Matt picked me up as easily as if I were a stuffed animal. Not that I know anything about them.

I was safe. My head ached. My shoulders were sore. I was shaking. But I wasn't sushi.

I heard Ava muttering, "He's gone. The shark . . ."

Leaning over the edge, Matt pointed down into the water below. "No, he's still here. He's about twenty feet down."

"We missed our chance," Maya said.

"No, we didn't," I answered.

"What do you mean?" Matt asked.

Look, I know this was a big moment, and they were right to be impatient, but I wanted to draw it out a little. When you live with geniuses, and the one new friend you make happens to be a genius of another kind, you have to enjoy your little moments of accomplishment. There are no medal stands in normal life, so you've got to make them for yourself. I was thinking about delivering a small speech when Ava darted in like an ultimate fighter and pried open my hand with her surprisingly strong fingers, revealing the prized tracking device.

My brother hugged me hard enough to shatter my ribs. My high five with Maya this time was slightly more successful. At least I didn't smack her in the head. I could have sworn I heard Ava say I was amazing or something, but by the time my head had cleared and my heart had stopped beating as fast as a hummingbird's wings, she'd moved past praise. She was already wiring the pressure sensor to the tracking device.

The island was far off to our right.

The sky was growing darker by the minute.

Before long, Ava was finished, and we were taking turns tapping out our S-O-S message in Morse code, alternating between three short beats, three longer ones, and another

227

trio of quick taps—hoping all the while that someone was watching. Rosa, maybe. Ashley. Hank. Even Steven.

The wind was blowing stronger, the sky growing darker.

Then Maya spotted something large flying away from the island in our direction. Only this was no red-footed booby.

"The underplane!" Ava yelled. "It's the underplane!"

"The underplane?" Maya asked. "Who builds a plane out of underwear?"

If I weren't so relieved, I would have laughed. And if Maya weren't there, I might have cried. "We're saved," I whispered.

Matt looked right and left. "Not yet," he said. "There's no way he's going to be able to land in these waves. The water's too choppy."

"But he sees us," I noted.

The plane approached. Hank was piloting the vehicle with the air-conditioning king sitting beside him. Inside, they were cheering and high-fiving, and on *Niu* we were whooping as loud as a stadium full of fans.

Maya pointed. Black smoke trailed behind the plane.

"That's not good," I said.

"No," Matt said quietly. "No, it's not."

"I don't even care," Maya said. "They know we're here."

Normally I'd pass on the chance to ride in an experimental

flying submarine with smoke spewing out the tail. But when you've been lost at sea for two days, eating raw fish and sleeping outside, wiping yourself with the remains of a blue blazer, your standards change. A rescue was a rescue. And I was getting on that plane.

"Why isn't he launching the chute?" Ava asked.

After looping past us, Hank must have noticed the smoke. He held up his index finger. "He's telling us to wait a minute," Matt guessed. "Maybe someone's on their way by boat."

Sure enough, the underplane turned back for Nihoa, and a little while later, we spotted the black hull and white spray of a boat speeding toward us. We couldn't tell if it was *Vader* or *Luthor*, and we didn't care. I reached into my pocket, laid my still-damp tie across my lap, and tried to flatten out the wrinkles before tying the bow.

"What are you doing?" Ava asked.

"I'm trying to fix myself up for the cameras."

"What cameras?"

Poor Matt. He understood galaxies. Planets. But not people. He knew how stars worked, but not celebrities. Four kids had been lost at sea for two days. Two, maybe even three of them were mildly famous. This would be huge news. In Hawaii, at the least. But probably worldwide. Back on Nihoa, news crews, bloggers, journalists, and adoring fans would be waiting with desperate requests for comments and stories. Autographs? I'd sign a few. Some of the journalists would no doubt have talked their way onto the rescue boat speeding our way. They'd have questions, too. Had we been scared? Did we ever think we'd die? Jack, they'd ask, where did you get that tie?

I like to be prepared. And so I wanted to look good. What's so strange about that? "Believe me, Matt," I said, finger-combing my hair to one side, "there will be cameras."

The boat approached.

My smile quickly faded.

There were no cameras.

There were no reporters.

Instead, a single person stood at the wheel. He wore dark sunglasses. His goatee was as thick as a pair of wool socks. And he was the last guy any of us wanted to see.

16
THE REAL SABOTEUR

ANY OF YOU KNOW KARATE?" MAYA ASKED.

Make that five times I wished I knew kung fu.

"What if we hide?" I asked.

"Seriously, Jack?" Ava said.

Fine, so that wasn't my best brainstorm.

"He can't do anything to us now," Matt said. "Hank knows we're here."

"So what do we do?"

"Think of it like a game of chess," Matt suggested.

"I don't play chess," I reminded him.

"We need to think several steps ahead."

"But first we need to see his initial move," Ava said. "Then we figure out how to counter."

His first move was not what I expected.

I doubt it was what any of us expected.

The thick and grizzled ex-SEAL cut *Vader*'s motor, tossed Maya a line, leaped over onto our raft, and wrapped me in a bear hug. At first I thought he was trying to kill me, and that this was some kind of military wrestling move. Briefly I considered biting him; according to my foster-care records, I was pretty good at this when I was a toddler. Besides, I couldn't think of any other escape. Then I realized he wasn't fighting me. Not even close. He was swinging me from side to side and laughing. For a second there, I kind of gave in to the embrace, and it was actually a really, really good hug. He stopped and gave me this look like I'd done something wrong, and then he tossed me to one side and hugged each of the equally shocked girls, lifting them both off their feet. Matt sort of flinched when Kildare approached him, so he threw his arm around Matt's shoulder instead, pulling him in for the one-armed guy version. Over and over, he kept saying how he couldn't believe that we'd made it back. "Your grandfather's waiting," he told Maya. "He's over the moon with excitement. But I'll give it to him—the guy had total and complete faith in you."

"He did?"

"Oh, sure," Kildare said. "He said you'd find your way. And you guys saw Hank, right?" We nodded. "The under-plane's having a little engine trouble, but they just radioed in that they touched down safely near the cove. They'll meet us on the beach with Ben." Shaking his head, he hugged me again, then slapped Matt on the shoulder. "I can't believe it. Amazing!"

My brother and I glanced at each other. Finally, Matt spoke up. "Why are you happy to see us? We know it was you. We followed you out to the lab."

"Me? What do you mean?"

"We know you sabotaged the project," Ava said. "You destroyed the lab."

I stared at my siblings, wishing we had telepathic powers. If we did, I would have mind-shouted at them, wondering what in the world they were doing. Confronting him directly, without other witnesses, didn't strike me as the smartest chess move. Sun Tzu probably wouldn't have liked the tactic, either.

233

Kildare grabbed a line from *Vader* and walked it up to *Niu*'s bow. "There was a terrible fire. The whole lab flooded and collapsed. Everything inside was ruined." He crouched at the front of the boat and started to tie off one end of the line. "But I didn't have anything to do with it."

"We saw you sneaking down to the lab two nights ago—"

"Sneaking? I wasn't sneaking anywhere." Kildare lifted his bearded chin in my direction. "I was following him. I was going to leave this for later, after we all got back to the house, but I'm not the suspect here. Everyone knows it's you who destroyed the lab, Jack."

"Me?"

"Steven said he saw you snooping around the fireworks at the party. His robot has it on video."

"That doesn't mean I—"

"Jack didn't do it," Maya said. "The four of us were together the whole time."

Kildare's eyes scrunched together. "I followed you all the way down to the beach."

"No," Ava said, slowly, as if she were explaining something to a kindergartner, "we followed you. You're the one who—"

Furious, the ex-SEAL threw the line down onto the deck. "I risked my life trying to put that fire out!" he said. "I could've been killed. Stop lying." He pointed one of his thick fingers at me. "Jack, I tracked your signal."

"What do you mean, my signal?"

"The cat!" Ava shouted.

"What cat?" Maya asked.

"Mr. Tinkles," Matt said definitively.

"Winkles," Kildare corrected. "You found the tracking device?" I nodded. Then he shrugged, unapologetic. "I needed to know where everyone was, for safety reasons. Plus I didn't trust you three." He pointed to me. "Especially not you."

"Good choice," Matt said, "but he's not the one you were tracking. They ditched the device right before the party."

234

"Then please explain to me who it was that snuck out of the party, motored out to the dock, set off those fireworks, and destroyed the lab?"

The answer was unlikely. In some ways it didn't even make sense. "Albert Charles Krumplitch," I said. "The air-conditioning king."

No reporters were waiting on the beach. No camera crews or bloggers, either. As we cruised toward the cove, towing the battered *Niu* behind us, a small crowd awaited us. The three of us were massively relieved to see Hank. Ashley stood with Steven, Clementine, Rosa, and a half-dozen others. Maya muttered something sarcastic about how her parents weren't there, but Ben was waiting at the water's edge, looking ready to swim out to greet her, and the rest of *Ohana*'s crew waited beside him. Krumplitch was on shore as well. "You'd think he would be gone by now," Matt said.

"No, he was just as worried as anyone," Kildare replied. "I don't think he had any idea you kids were out there that night."

"Plus he has no clue we know he's behind it," Ava noted.

"Let's keep it that way for now," Kildare said. "I don't think you four need any more excitement today."

The wind pushed harder at our backs, as if the approaching storm were trying to hurry us to safety. Hank and Ben and David all rushed out into waist-deep water and climbed up onto the boat before it reached the beach, wrapping us in one sea-drenched hug after another. Steven clapped his hands to the side of his head, then swept them behind his back and watched us from a distance. When we finally stepped foot on the beach, I kneeled down and kissed the sand. I wouldn't recommend that, though. It took me a full minute to clean off my lips.

Rosa embraced each of us, and I caught my sister smiling when the engineer pulled her close, but Ava wriggled free after about two seconds. The air-conditioning king and the tattooed chef wrapped their arms around us, too, so by the time Ashley stood in front of me, I was pretty much hugged out. Luckily, she's even more allergic to affection than Ava. She pointed at me and embraced the empty space in front of her. I guess you'd call it an air-hug. Strangely enough, it was kind of nice.

Ben wouldn't leave Maya's side, and after handing her a phone so she could talk to her parents, who were not terribly happy with her grandfather, he kept saying how proud he was of her. The geniuses, meanwhile, wouldn't let go of Hank's attention. Ava was showing him and Rosa the S-O-S shoe—Hank called it a brilliant solution, but said it didn't look very comfortable—and Matt couldn't stop talking about all the stars he'd seen. At one point, Hank realized that Matt had missed his test, and he offered to contact his professor about getting him an extension. My brother said he didn't even care, and that response froze our mentor's brain. Hank looked to me for an explanation. "What happened out there?" he asked.

I shrugged. "Everything."

Thankfully someone mentioned food, and we started walking up the hill to the main house. I brought up a story Hank had told us once, about how when astronauts return from long trips to space, people actually carry them out of their ships because they're too weak to walk.

"How is that relevant?" Steven asked, practically spitting out the question.

"Anyone want to carry me?"

They all laughed.

I wasn't joking.

After a long, slow trudge up the path, and a sudden sprint to the nearest bathroom, I joined the others in the eat-in kitchen. The square counter was crowded with food and drinks, and the chef kept rushing out from the main kitchen with more. I was chugging water and feasting on ham-and-cheese-stuffed sandwiches and freshly baked chocolate chip cookies. Someone put a mug full of hot beef broth in front of me. At one point, I dunked a cookie into the soup without thinking, then ate it anyway.

237

Steven wasn't even bothering to hide his disgust at my eating choices, but his mother was struggling to resist the desserts. At least three times I saw her reach for a chocolate chip cookie, then pull her hand back and grab an asparagus spear from the plate of raw vegetables instead.

Hank was unusually affectionate. Ava slipped out of three of his hugs before finally giving in to one. A second later, though, he pulled away to dig his phone out of his pocket. After glancing at the screen, he handed it to me. "Here," he said, "tell Min you're safe."

Normally Min is pretty calm and cool. But when I said hello, she practically shrieked with joy. "And the others?" she asked. "Matthew? Ava? They're both fine?"

"Totally fine," I said. "Matthew has this weird mark on his forehead now, and I think Ava's shorter, but otherwise they're good." While my brother got up from the counter to look for a mirror, I noticed Hawaiian music in the background. "Min, is that a luau? Where are you?" My mood dropped like an elevator that just had its cable clipped when she explained. Apparently she panicked when Hank told her we were missing, and he bought her a ticket to Hawaii. "I had to go first class," she said. "There were no other seats left." And then when she finally got to Hawaii, she couldn't find anyone to fly her to Nihoa because of the weather, so she had to wait at the Green Room Resort.

"The place with the twenty-four-hour ice cream bar, right?" I asked.

"Yes. Did you know they have twenty-five different toppings, too?"

I did. "The hotel with five different pools?"

"That's the one," Min said. "But I'll be there to join you as soon as I can."

I handed Ava the phone.

My siblings each spoke with her briefly, and then we resumed eating like a professional football team. Eventually, our little welcome-back party started to thin. Clementine slipped away. The *Ohana* crew said their good-nights and returned to their camp in the cove. Maya and her grandfather remained, though—Ashley insisted she stay in the house, and her grandfather wanted to stay close to her.

Hank, Rosa, Ben, and Ashley were desperate to know how we'd survived. The king hung around, too, but he seemed more interested in the food than anything else. My sister sat next to Rosa and talked more about her homemade rescue shoe.

Between bites, we told them all about the celestial navigation, the SpiderStretch laces, and our fishing success. Hank didn't even bother correcting Matt's manners when my brother was describing the path of tana mun through the sky and chewing a piece of cold steak at the same time. And

239

you could actually hear the meaty mush moving around in his mouth. Even I was grossed out.

Still, we never really got to the center of the story. Every time someone asked why we were heading out to the lab in the first place, Kildare would cut in. "We can talk about all that in the morning," he'd insist.

I was thinking about going for a sixth chocolate chip cookie when the air-conditioning king excused himself with an island-shaking yawn. "I must have my beauty rest," he explained. "Shall we all reconvene tomorrow?"

As he shuffled away, proclaiming how happy he was to see us alive, I noticed that the prince was no longer with us, either. "Where'd Steven go?" I asked Matt.

"He would be in his lab now," Ashley said. Her expression brightened. "Einstein liked to work at night, too."

The door swung shut. My brother ignored her and addressed Kildare. "We're still going to wait for the morning?"

"We don't have to. If you're game, now is as good a time as any," the ex-SEAL replied.

"For what?" Ashley asked.

Ava cracked her knuckles. "To tell you all the truth."

17
CRIMINALLY SHAPED

I LOOKED AROUND THE ROOM. THE FOUR OF US REMAINED, plus Hank, Ashley, Rosa, Ben, and Kildare. Oh, and Harriet, apparently. The robot had rolled into the room at some point. I hadn't noticed. But now the silver machine was positioned near the door, against the wall, with its two electronic eyes facing the group. Something about the robot scared me. There was no use in saying anything to Ava or Matt. They'd make fun of me. They'd attempt to explain away my fears in terms of codes or wiring. But something about Harriet was unnatural. I don't believe in ghosts. Or not really. But I could've sworn that robot was possessed.

Ashley let out a frustrated growl when she noticed Harriet. "That thing is everywhere," she complained. "That's the last time

I get my son a two-hundred-thousand-dollar robot for his birthday."

My sister looked as if she was going to faint. She mouthed the sum to me. "Two hundred thousand?"

"So?" Hank asked. "What is the truth? What's this mysterious secret you're harboring?"

Once Matt and Ava summarized what we knew, and why we thought Krumplitch was the real saboteur, Rosa hurled her pen across the room. Ashley kept repeating, "Really? Really?" And her tone changed each time, moving back and forth between disbelief and genuine curiosity.

Our mentor silently circled the room, drumming his fingers on his chin. Behind Matt's chair, he stopped, held out his right pinky and jabbed it forward as he asked, "Why?"

242

"Why?" Ashley repeated.

"Why," Hank said, "would Albert want to sabotage the underwater lab?"

Rosa collected her mangled pen from the floor, rinsed it in the sink and dried it on the bottom of her shirt. She was standing below a vent on the wall. She paused, held her face up to the cool air, then gasped. "Wait. Wait!"

"For what?" Hank asked.

Ava eyed the vent, then pointed to Rosa, excited. "I know!"

I glanced over at Hank. First the smiles. Now it was like they were best friends.

"What do you think?" Rosa pressed.

"Well, in addition to clean energy, the TOES also produces cool air."

"And cold water," Matt added, needing to chip in.

"Right, but that's not important," Ava said, her words coming out in a rush. "The cool air could be another form of air-conditioning."

"We've already talked to a few resorts on the big island about installing test systems," Ashley said. "They wouldn't even need normal air-conditioning anymore."

"Which wouldn't be great news for the king," Maya noted.

"The TOES could ruin his business," Hank said.

The bazillionaire picked up my soup and sipped from the top. "This coffee is terrible," she said.

"That's beef broth," I noted.

She spun and spat into the sink.

"How much would he lose?" Hank asked.

Ashley rocked her head back and forth. "He has the contracts for all the big hotels and office buildings on the islands," she said. "If the TOES proved effective, then everyone around here would want it. Cheap, clean energy? Why wouldn't they?"

Maya repeated Hank's question. "But how much would he lose?"

243

"Millions, most likely."

"Millions of dollars?" I asked. "Really?"

Ashley shrugged. "Sure," she said, "maybe more."

Believe me, I didn't like the king. Not at all. But I couldn't help feeling a little blip of sympathy for anyone who lost that much money, criminal or not.

Ashley grabbed the mug of coffee in front of Hank, swished some around inside her mouth, then put it back down in front of him. He stared down at the cup as she thought aloud. To the adults, she added, "But it's not like he meant to drown the kids, right? He didn't know they were going to be outside the lab."

No. Probably not. But that didn't make me feel better.

Hank pushed his tainted mug to the center of the counter. "The damage at the base of the pipe still puzzles me. How did he do it?"

Harriet wheeled closer to the counter. I stood up and walked to the opposite side. From my new seat, I noticed Kildare watching Ashley, as if he was waiting for permission. She flicked the fingers of her right hand toward him. "I can explain," he said. "I looked into some of those vehicles we talked about after the incident. Remember that underwater tour guide who normally operates out of Kauai? First of all, he has a record. Robbing bakeries, mostly. Small-time money. An apparent preference for powdered donuts, too. And it turns out he was gone for three days right around the time the pipe was sabotaged. He didn't return my calls or emails at first, but he finally got back to me when you four were lost at sea, and I got him to talk."

A chill coursed through my spine as I imagined the terrifying techniques Kildare must have used to force the confession. Would he go for the toenails? Maybe a gradual, painful plucking of the eyelashes? Or would he use some far more tortuous method? Personally, I'd be an easy subject. Just bake a tray full of chocolate chip cookies, pull it out of the oven while the chips are still gooey, then hold it near my nose. Offer me one of those cookies in exchange for information, and I'd tell you anything.

Kildare's methods probably weren't so delectable, though. I shivered. The ex-SEAL must have guessed what I was thinking. He held up his hands. "Whoa, Jack! It's not like I hurt him or anything. I just sent him two hundred bucks through PayPal and promised not to tell the cops."

"That would have worked for me, too," Maya said.

"I'd take an iTunes gift card," Ava added.

"So what did he say?" Hank pressed.

"He said someone offered him ten times his normal rate to go down and do the job. But he never met the person. Never even spoke to them on the phone."

"So we don't know it was the king," I said.

"No," Rosa said, "but he'd have the money."

Harriet turned slightly to face the engineer.

Across the table, Maya whispered to me, "That thing's creepy, right?"

"I still haven't figured out how Krumplitch could've gotten into the lab two nights ago," Kildare said. "He'd need to know the code to open the door."

"I didn't tell him," Rosa said.

"Did any of you write the code down somewhere?" Ava asked. "On a Post-it note, maybe?"

Ashley was silent for a second. "How'd you know that?"

Ava shrugged as if the answer was obvious. "Old people always write their passwords on Post-it notes."

"I am not old!" Ashley insisted.

"But you wrote it down on a note?"

The bazillionaire stared down at the counter and nodded.

"He did the same thing," Ava added, pointing to Kildare. Then, to me, she explained, "That's how I unlocked the shark tracking app, to show you how he was using it to follow us, too."

Impressed, Rosa patted Ava on the back, and my sister smiled proudly. The embarrassed ex-SEAL covered his face with his hands.

"You're supposed to be my security chief," Ashley exclaimed.

Kildare shrugged. "I'm forgetful."

Rosa tapped her pen on the counter. "How did he get out? Kildare, you said you were trying to put out the fire. You would've seen someone, right?"

"Absolutely," he answered. "The only way out without being seen would have been down through the moon pool. But from there it's about a hundred feet to the surface."

"Which would be impossible," Ashley said.

"Not if you had SCUBA gear," Hank noted.

"There wasn't enough time for him to get into SCUBA gear," Kildare replied.

After a few seconds of silence, Maya spoke up. "What if he swam? Could you hold your breath for that long, Grandfather?"

Ben shrugged. "A hundred feet? It's not easy, but sure."

I'd forgotten that her grandfather was a former free diver.

Matt leaned his elbows on the marble counter. "He doesn't look like he's in shape for that."

Hank suddenly stood as straight as a ruler, like he'd been struck by some kind of mental lightning bolt. "Ah, but that's where you're wrong!" he declared. He pulled a marker out of his pocket, moved to the wall, and drew the figure of a walrus. "He's the perfect shape."

"You forgot the whiskers," I noted.

Hank sneered, but added them. Then he sketched a

cartoonish but surprisingly accurate version of the king right beside the whiskered swimmer. "See, Mr. Krumplitch's body type is actually rather hydrodynamic, like that of a walrus. The small head, the narrow shoulders, gradually tapering outward to a wide waistline, and down again to narrow legs. The water flows right around them both beautifully."

"Fascinating," Rosa remarked.

"That's not one of the whiteboard walls," Ashley noted.

Hank swiped at the drawing with his thumb. It didn't smudge. "Oh. Sorry."

The bazillionaire quickly thumb-typed on her phone. Without looking up, she added, "It's fine, I'll have someone paint it."

"Anyway, I wasn't talking about his actual shape," Matt said. "I was talking about his fitness. He doesn't look like he's in good enough shape to hold his breath for ten seconds."

Maya's grandfather slapped his hand on the counter. A plate bounced slightly, and one of the chocolate chip cookies fell off and over the edge. I caught it on the top of my foot before it hit the floor. Sadly, no one noticed.

"I know him!" Ben said.

"Trust me, it's the ads," Maya said.

"No, no." Ben covered his eyes with his right hand and made a small, frustrated, groaning sound. "Lanai, maybe? No, Oahu. A contest there. Twenty-two, twenty-three years ago. Maybe more. I'd already retired, but I still followed the events. He placed third to Dommage, the French champion. I believe he dove eighty meters."

Ava made a clicking sound with her tongue, then added, "That's two hundred and sixty-two feet."

"Two hundred and sixty-three," Ashley said. "You have to round up."

"Well, actually, it's two hundred and sixty-two point four six seven," Matt said. "So you're kind of both right."

I smiled over at Maya. Had she ever seen a geek fight before? This was a good one.

"That's enough," Hank said.

"If I'm right, and he once dove that deep," Ben said, "he could still surface from a hundred feet down. Easily."

"So he steals the code, drives out—"

"He'd need to steal the boat key, too," I noted.

"Right," Kildare continued. "So he steals the key, takes the boat, sets off the fireworks, then he sees or hears me coming and swims out through the moon pool."

"But how do we prove it?" Ava asked. "Even if everything lines up, we don't have any proof."

Rosa nodded in agreement. "A theory is nothing without data."

"We could always confront him," I suggested. Then I motioned to the adults. "Or you guys could, anyway."

Before anyone had time to respond, the door swung open, and the air-conditioning king himself stepped through into the kitchen. The room was as quiet as a cave. Kildare was frozen, holding a cookie just above his chin. Hank slid along the wall to cover his cartoon. Rosa was glaring at the king so angrily that I wouldn't have been surprised if red laser beams suddenly shot out of her eyes. Even Harriet turned to face him.

The king walked casually over to the fridge, removed two of Steven's precious cheese sticks, peeled away the plastic, and bit off a chunk. He started moving back toward the door. "Carry on, carry on," the king said. "Don't let me interrupt. Just a little snack before bed." No one spoke. He stopped, chewing. "What? What's wrong?" he asked. "Why's everyone looking at me?"

Maybe the silence was intentional, and they were planning to accuse him later, after we'd come up with a plan. Or maybe no one was sure who was supposed to speak first. So I took that job. I shuffled closer to Kildare, just to be safe. "We know everything, Krumplitch," I said, spitting out his name like it was a rotten sunflower seed. "The sabotage, the moon pool, the challenge to your air-conditioning empire. We know you're behind it all."

Unexpectedly, Maya joined me. "You may as well confess."

"Tell us the truth, Albert," Rosa pleaded.

The king backed toward the door. Eyes wide, face pale, Albert Charles Krumplitch pointed his partially eaten cheese stick at Ashley Hawking and cried, "She made me do it!"

18
THE ART OF WAR

CHAOS? YES, I GUESS THAT'S THE RIGHT WORD FOR what happened next. You could also call it pandemonium. Conversational madness. Complete social disorder. The king was pointing his cheese stick at Ashley and shouting like a first grader trying to shift the blame for a playground fight. The bazillionaire was laughing one moment, shouting angrily the next, and all the while insisting she had absolutely nothing to do with the sabotage. Rosa was livid. At one point she yelled that she didn't care which one of them was behind it all as long as someone told the truth. Kildare was calmly trying to defuse the situation. He was still holding on to that cookie, too. Ben, meanwhile, seemed amused by the whole mess, and Hank was watching everyone like a zoologist observing a family of mountain gorillas in the jungle.

Krumplitch's story was simple. He claimed that a few weeks earlier, he'd received an email from Ashley outlining the threat the TOES posed to his air-conditioning empire. She wrote that she'd made a mistake in funding the project and that she wanted to see it fail. Naturally, he'd asked why, and she'd said there were tax-related reasons. To be perfectly honest, I didn't really understand that part. Ava might have, since she always did our taxes, and she nodded in a knowing sort of way.

Anyway, then Krumplitch said Ashley gave him the idea to pay the submarine operator to sabotage the pipe. "You still owe me that money, by the way."

"What money?" Ashley asked.

"The money I paid, out of my own account, to that donut-loving crook!" the king shouted, ejecting thin showers of spit with each word. "Not to mention the fee for destroying the lab."

"What fee? I literally have no idea what you're talking about!"

In a low voice, Ava said, "You almost killed us."

The king held his hands together and faced us. "I didn't mean to, honestly," he pleaded. "You weren't supposed to be there. I didn't even know you'd been to the lab until I got back to the house. And I did all I could to help find you once we realized you were lost."

"But why did you do it?" Rosa asked. "Do you have any idea how hard I worked on that system?"

253

"You? How hard you worked? Your invention could have shattered my empire!" the king said. "I spent my whole life building my air-conditioning business."

Ashley's left eye closed halfway as she said, "You inherited it from your mother."

The king swept his hands in the air like he was shooing away a storm of flies. "Inherited, built . . . minor details! The point is that I wasn't going to let it crumble."

Rosa asked her next question through clenched teeth. "How much did she pay you?"

"I didn't pay him!"

"How much?" Rosa repeated.

"She offered me two hundred thousand dollars," the king said. "Not a lot, but nothing to scoff at, either. And I'm still waiting for the funds."

That wasn't much? I'd buy a limousine. With an ice-cream machine inside. And maybe a robot to drive me around.

"Prove it," Ashley insisted.

And he did. Or at least he tried to, anyway. Ashley made Krumplitch show everyone the supposed emails on his phone. Then she claimed that the address was a fake. "Who even has a Yahoo! account anymore?" she asked. "This is ridiculous!"

"Yes," Rosa said. She turned to Ashley. "You're right. This is ridiculous, and I think you're lying."

"He's lying!" Ashley insisted.

"Someone's lying," Rosa said.

Ashley pointed to the king. "I should have you arrested."

"Arrested?" The king laughed. His jowls quivered. "Who, exactly, is going to arrest me? There are no police here. Besides, I don't believe that destruction of private property is a crime if the owner of the property offers to pay you. That's called business."

"For the last time, I didn't offer you anything!"

As she watched the redhead's temper rise, Maya said to me, "See? Pele, the fire goddess."

The king started to leave, but Kildare blocked his way. "Kindly move, sir." The ex-SEAL watched Ashley, waiting for orders. "You can't keep me here," the king insisted. "If you wish to sue me, feel free, but my daughter and I are leaving this island at the first opportunity."

255

A reluctant nod from Ashley prompted Kildare to step aside, and the king stormed out. The rest of us simply sat there for a minute, stunned and confused. The denials and accusations hung in the air like smoke.

Ashley climbed off her stool, but Rosa shook her finger at the bazillionaire. "No, no, no. You're not slipping away. I want the truth."

Hank leaned forward, placed his hands flat on the counter, and looked at each of us kids in turn. "As for you four, though," he began, "I think this is a good time to get some rest."

Matt started to protest, insisting that he wanted to be a part of the discussion, but his words quickly transformed into a massive yawn. His sleepy roar proved contagious, spreading quickly to Ava, Maya, and yours truly. My eyes teared up. "Maybe you're right," Matt admitted.

The four of us dragged ourselves out of the kitchen and up the stairs. Ben confessed to Maya that he hadn't slept for two nights because he'd been so worried. And I was so ridiculously exhausted that I had to pause halfway up to unleash a few more yawns. "You coming?" Matt asked.

"In a second," I said.

We said our good-nights, and when they turned the corner, someone behind me called my name.

I turned. At the bottom of the stairs, Clementine held a finger to her lips. She hurried quietly up. "Where's Ava?" she asked. "I need to tell her something."

"She's in her room." The girl was working really hard to avoid eye contact. She was hiding something. "What is it?" I asked. "You can tell me."

Looking down at her bare feet, she began, "My father . . . what he did . . ." She rolled her head in a circle as if she were watching a Ferris Wheel. "I'm not making excuses."

"No?"

"No," she whispered. Finally, she looked at me directly. "Then what are you doing?"

She pointed to the second-floor hallway. "What you guys were saying in there about the robot being kind of weird—"

"You were listening?"

"I'm always listening," she replied with a shrug. "Anyway, I think it might be time for you to listen. Up there," she finished, nodding her head toward the top of the stairs.

I turned to see what she was pointing at, and when I spun back, Clementine had vanished.

Okay, so that's not quite true. She was just a few steps farther down the stairs, but when I called quietly to her, asking for an explanation, she kept moving. So I followed her advice. At the top of the stairs, a faint blue light was shining out from underneath the door to Steven's lab. I heard voices, too. Was that Hank? Yes. And Ashley's voice, too. Crouching down to the floor, I moved my left ear closer to the gap. The argument in the kitchen was still going on downstairs— they hadn't moved up here to Steven's lab. They would've had to pass us on the stairs. On the other side of the door, I heard whispers. But they were coming from people who were actually inside the room. I glanced down the empty hall, wishing my brother or sister or Maya were there with me. But the lights in their rooms were already out. Pressing my ear close to the door again, I picked out two voices. Two

257

people inside. And one of them was Steven Hawking. "Keep recording," he said, "I'll review it all in the morning."

His soft footsteps approached.

I rolled away and scurried back around the corner to the top of the stairs. The door opened, then clicked shut. A few seconds later, I heard a similar click. He'd gone into his room. I hurried back into the hall and knocked lightly on the lab door. Just loud enough for the person inside to hear, but no one else. I hoped.

The door opened. The wild-haired woman with the rectangular glasses rubbed her forehead and asked, "Did you forget your—"

Her face paled when she saw me. She tried to shut the door, but I slipped my foot through. The metal crushed the side of my ankle. I stifled a scream. She winced, then mouthed, "Sorry!" Yet she still tried to shut me out. I shoved my way through and closed the door behind me.

"You shouldn't be in here," she said. Her voice was low but urgent, and she kept glancing around me, as if she were expecting him to return.

Two overstuffed bookshelves lined the walls to my left and right. Across from the door, two posters were taped above a wide steel desk. One featured Albert Einstein, the other C-3PO. The picture of the famous golden droid looked ready to fall. The top right corner wasn't quite stuck to the wall. Below the posters, three computer monitors were positioned on the clean desk. The screen on the left was filled with lines of yellow numbers and letters against a black background. The one on the right showed a radar image of the local weather. And the center monitor included what appeared to be a live video feed of the kitchen. The view was centered on Rosa and Hank. Their voices were coming out of a thin rectangular speaker on the desk, and they were still discussing Krumplitch. The woman stood in front of the center screen, blocking my view. "You're not supposed to be in here," she said again.

"Neither are you."

"Yes, I am," she said. "I'm his tutor."

"His tutor?"

She opened her mouth to reply, then stopped and sat back in a desk chair. "Kind of his assistant, really," she said. "But I hate to admit that. I have a PhD in computer science, you know."

I didn't know that. I didn't know anything about this woman, except that her hair was funny looking. "Let's start over," I said. "I'm Jack."

"I know," she said. "Martha."

We were only an arm's length away, but she waved instead

259

of offering to shake my hand. I grabbed the only other chair in the room and sat across from Martha, facing the monitors. Now the screen in the middle featured a view of Ashley and Kildare. He was eating another cookie. Or was that the same cookie he'd been holding earlier? I pointed to the screen. "So where's the hidden camera? How are you getting those images?" She didn't answer, but she didn't need to answer. There were no hidden cameras in the room. The cameras had been right there in front of us the whole time. "Wait . . . is it Harriet?"

"Who's Harriet?"

"The robot," I said. "The HR-5 has been watching us?"

Martha ran her finger across the top of her eyeglasses. "Maybe?"

No wonder I'd felt creeped-out. "What do you mean, 'maybe'?"

"Well, it's not really the robot," she said. "It's more me. And Steven."

Hank was on the screen again. "So that's the view from the robot's eyes?"

Martha was nervously rolling a pencil around her fingers. For a moment I was mesmerized. I've always wanted to learn that trick. Then she looked back over her shoulder. "Yes," she said, "that's the view from the HR-5's cameras." She pointed her thumb at the speaker. "We're listening through its microphones, too."

The view shifted back to Ashley. She was staring directly

into the cameras now, and sighing with frustration. "I said, 'What is the weather forecast for the next three days?'" Ashley asked.

Frantically, Martha spun in her chair. She speed-typed on the keyboard. A new weather chart popped up on the screen to her right. She scanned the information, then rapidly typed out a few sentences. Through the speaker I heard the robot responding to Ashley's question. "The storm will continue through Sunday morning, with winds of forty-three miles per hour and gusts of sixty."

I leaned forward. That exact phrase appeared on the monitor to the left in bright yellow letters. "Wait, that was you?" I asked. Again Martha bit her lip. "So how does it work? You hear what the robot hears, and then the robot says whatever you type?"

"Pretty much," she said. "I'm the robot's brain. I drive it around a little, too."

"So that night at Steven's party . . . you were outside but then you ran."

"Yeah, because we didn't know Ashley was going to have him do a demonstration. So I had to get back up here to control everything."

"So Steven's not a coding wizard?"

She shook her head. "No. The HR-5 has some intelligence of its own, but that's all my work."

"For example?"

261

"Well, Steven always wants to know what everyone is saying about him, so I wrote a little program that has the robot roll closer to people and record their conversations when his name is mentioned. He asked me to add a few other topics, too. Rosa. The TOES. Your names. Well, really just Ava and Matt." That stung a little. "Then, if he's not here in the lab, he can listen to what was said later." She shrugged again when she saw my reaction. "I know. It's weird."

"Does Ashley know?"

Her eyes bulged. "No way. You can't tell her, either. Ashley hired me to tutor him in computer science, engineering, a few other subjects. But he pays me extra to keep the secret."

I rolled my chair closer to the desk and watched the adults in the kitchen. "Why? Why does he need to listen to everyone?"

"The same reason he wants his mom and everyone else to believe that he's a coding genius. He's insecure. He wants to live up to everyone's expectations."

That would explain why he wanted to hear what people were saying about him, too. Part of me even understood that. I almost felt bad for him. Almost. "But why the TOES? Why Rosa?" I asked.

Martha shrugged, but the moment I voiced the question, I knew the answer. I stood up and circled the small room. Even if he wasn't some kind of computer coding super genius, he was crafty enough to cook up a scheme that led everyone to believe that myth. To me, that was almost more impressive. Closer to my kind of intelligence.

He knew the submarine tour guide. He'd bragged about going for a trip with the guy.

He hated the island.

He was jealous of Rosa.

He wanted the TOES to fail.

"He did it," I said, more to myself than to Martha. "Steven is behind it all!"

"Shh! What are you talking about?"

Clementine had even said she wasn't sure why Steven had invited her to his birthday party in the first place. They'd only met once. And he hadn't even spoken to her. But he didn't want her at his party. He wanted her dad. "Steven's the one who arranged for Krumplitch to be here. He devised this whole scheme."

"The TOES? Steven? I don't think he's that—"

Outside in the hall, a door opened. Quick footsteps followed. Martha grabbed me by the shirt, pulled me up out of the chair, and shoved me back against the wall beside the door. Then it swung open and I stood crammed into the small space. In the crack between the hinges, I could just see the edge of Steven's profile. He was wearing

263

Superman pajamas. I would've guessed he'd be more of an Iron Man kid.

"Is everything okay?" Martha asked. Her voice sounded awkward, full of fake cheer.

"I just want to make sure you're recording," he answered. His voice was low, just louder than a whisper. "This is important."

"I'm recording."

"You're sure?"

"I'm sure," Martha insisted.

"You better be," he said, "because I can always find another tutor."

The door slammed. The rush of air caught the C-3PO poster across the room and the upper right corner came loose, folding back over itself. The poster had been covering something. I pulled it down, revealing a blueprint of the TOES taped to the wall. Next to that, a copy of an article in the *Honolulu Times* about the air-conditioning king. Everything was there. All the proof I needed. "I need to go," I said.

Martha grabbed my shoulder. "Wait," she said. "You can't tell him I told you anything. A few more months with the little devil and my student loans will be paid off. Please don't mess this up for me, okay?"

"I'm not going to tell him you told me anything," I said. "I'm going to get him to confess on his own."

• • •

Sure, that sounded great. I'd get Steven to admit to everything without getting his tutor in trouble. There was just the small matter of how I was going to make this happen. I went to my brother and sister for help, but Matt was snoring like a rhinoceros with a sinus infection, and Ava was sleeping so heavily that I actually held a little mirror over her mouth to make sure she was breathing. Watching them rest brought back my yawning fit, and I quickly abandoned my plans to plot against Steven Hawking in favor of a little nap. I figured I'd just lie down for a little while, then wake up and spend all night crafting a brilliant scheme. Einstein worked at night? Well, then, I would, too. I'd stand at the window, in the darkness, looking down at the violent ocean far below, and develop the perfect strategy.

Instead, I just slept.

For fourteen hours.

By the time I finally forced myself out of that luxurious bed, my mind was still foggy, but I was pretty sure I'd dreamed about narwhals. Or elephants. Maybe a combination of the two? Yes, and with my head still crowded with narphants and elephals, I grabbed my backpack, threw in my copy of *The Art of War* for inspiration, and headed out into the hall.

My siblings were no longer in their rooms. Maya and Ben had cleared out, too—their beds were made. Downstairs was empty, but I found the chef. After a large, late breakfast

265

of pancakes with slightly runny fried eggs on top—so that the yolk leaks onto each bite, mingling with the butter and syrup—I walked outside in search of the others. Matt, Ava, and Maya were coming up the hill from the south side of the island. The wind was insanely strong and uneven. A light rain had begun to fall. Their leisurely walk turned into a jog. When they reached the house, they were soaked. Maya's hair looked different, too—and not just from the rain. Had she combed it?

"Jack?" Ava said. "Jack?"

I blinked a few times and rubbed my eyes. Maybe that way she'd think I wasn't staring. Then I noticed their expressions. They were concerned. Disappointed about something. Once he recovered his breath from the run, Matt's shoulders hung low and lifeless. "Sorry," I said. "What's wrong?"

"Krumplitch is gone," Matt said.

"Clementine, too," Maya added. "They took *Luthor* late last night, before the storm really picked up."

"It doesn't matter," I said.

"What? Why not?" Ava asked.

Matt continued past me into the house. The rest of us followed, and I was about to tell them what I'd learned about Steven when Harriet spun to face us.

"Jack, why are you smiling?" Maya asked.

Why? Because I had an idea. A beautiful idea.

"I found out more about the TOES," I said, pronouncing that last word with extra emphasis. The robot didn't move. "You know what I'm talking about, right? The Thermal Ocean Energy System"—I raised my voice again—"also known as TOES?"

Ava looked at me like my brain was the size of a grape. "Yes, Jack, we know about the TOES."

Now the robot reacted. Harriet's motors whirred as she wheeled toward us. All because Ava spoke. The little prince was probably in his lab listening to us at that very moment. But I didn't want him to hear everything. Not yet. We were fishing, and I was about to offer my first little piece of bait. "I think I know who really sabotaged the TOES," I said, "but I can't tell you here. Let's go somewhere private."

267

Harriet followed us, but the robot climbed stairs about as quickly as a grandma with a broken leg. In Matt's room, I closed the door and pressed my finger to my lips.

"What was that all about, Jack?" Matt asked.

I pointed to my sister. "You were right, Ava. What you said that night at the birthday party. This whole time, Steven has been pulling a Turkish delight."

"What's that?" Maya asked.

"He's been remote-controlling the robot. Steven and his tutor, Martha." They looked at me like I was talking about elephals and narphants. "You know, the lady with the crazy hair and the glasses?"

My sister's expression changed from forehead-wrinkling curiosity to raw, smiling glee. She clenched both her fists and shook them slowly. She was like a just-ignited firecracker of joy, ready to explode into bursts of happy light. My brother, on the other hand, was laughing. "It's a Mechanical Turk," he said. "Turkish delights are a kind of candy."

"They taste a lot like Swedish Fish, which, by the way, are manufactured in Turkey."

I spun around. Hank silently shut the door behind him. "How did you do that?" I asked. "The door was closed. You're like a ninja."

"Not really. I'm terrible with swords. But I suppose I do have a facility for quiet. Some years ago I spent a week in a sleep-research laboratory. Interesting study. Several inventors agreed to be subjects. The effects of REM sleep on creative productivity. Anyway, we were asked to sleep as much as possible and to make as little noise as possible." He shrugged. "Another participant complained about the slightest sounds. Ever since then I can cross a room as silently as a mouse. I even learned to silence my . . ." He glanced from me to Maya. "Never mind." Hank sat back against Matt's desk and smiled. "It really is so good to see you three—excuse me, four—back here safely. Now, what sort of scheme are you concocting?"

"We're not scheming," I lied.

Hank leaned forward. "Then why are we whispering?"

"It's a long story," I said.

"And we're still waiting to hear it all," Maya said. A little vein of frustration ran through her response.

"Does it have to do with the HR-5 stationed outside your door?"

The others looked to me. "Yes, it does."

"Steven has been faking his demonstrations with the robot," Ava explained.

"And that's not all," I added. "He has been using her to spy on everyone and listen to their conversations."

"Why?" Hank asked.

"Because he's the mastermind behind the whole plot to destroy the TOES."

269

"Wait," Matt said, "what?"

Ava let out a small, skeptical laugh. "Steven? No way."

"Jack," Hank added, "don't be ridiculous. That's absurd!"

I pointed to the door, reminding him to be quiet. "Just let me explain, okay?"

And he did. See, that's the thing about Hank. He responds to data. He'll happily change his mind on a topic if you have clear evidence. This was an essential characteristic for any decent scientist, according to Hank—and he said it wasn't a bad quality for a regular person, either. Sure, his belief in the power of data could be annoying. Like if he were to find that his private stash of chocolates in the lab had been emptied, and then he were to notice that someone had a smear of chocolate on the side of his—or her—mouth. But this time his belief in the power of evidence was welcome. I told them everything I knew, then made them swear to uphold my promise to protect Martha.

When I was finished, Ava was giddy. "We have to tell Rosa," she said.

Matt was quietly mulling, and Maya confessed that she was impressed with the spoiled prince. She just couldn't figure out why he was so rude to her family when they shared the same goal. Meanwhile, Hank stared at the ceiling for a full ten seconds before declaring in a hushed tone, "Yes, that is puzzling. So, Jack," he said, "did you collect the evidence?"

That would have been smart. "Well, I . . ."

Maya made the shape of a phone with her hands. "You took a picture at least, right?"

"No, I was . . . I wasn't thinking."

"Jack, come on," Matt said, his voice growing frustratingly loud. "Are you serious?"

Thankfully, Hank was there to defuse him. "There has to be another way. You could get back in the room, right?"

I shrugged. "Maybe."

"Or you could try to get him to confess," Hank suggested. "That would really be best for everyone."

"But how would we do that?" Maya asked.

"We could threaten to tell his mom the truth about the robot," Ava offered.

Hank shook his head, his mouth twisted as if he'd just tasted something sour. "Threaten. Such a terrible word. I could also talk to his mother—"

All four of us replied, "No!"

"Okay, okay," Hank said. "But I'm not entirely comfortable sitting here plotting against a thirteen-year-old boy."

I looked at the others, then Hank. "So we can't do anything?"

"No! I'm not saying that," Hank said. "You're young. He's young. Plot and plan away. I'd just prefer not to be such an obvious accomplice. Please remember, though. He is human. He has a heart, and I don't mean the four-chambered engine of his circulatory system."

"We don't want to hurt him. We just want him to tell the truth."

Only after I said that did I realize it was actually true.

Once Hank was gone, I pulled my copy of *The Art of War* from my backpack and flipped to a line I'd read the night before my submarine trip with Ashley. "Here," I said, handing the book to Matt. "Chapter one, verse eighteen."

271

My brother ran his finger along the page, nodding, as Maya and Ava read over his shoulder. "All warfare is based on deception," he said. "So are you saying we should trick him?"

Maya took the book and scanned the page. "Another verse here says that if your enemy has a temper, you should irritate him. Should we take his cheese sticks or something?"

Ava grimaced. "This isn't really an accurate translation."

"You read Chinese?" Maya asked.

"A little."

"Forget the translation," I said, "and the cheese sticks. There's one thing he'd hate more than someone stealing his food."

Matt tilted his head to one side. "What's that?"

"Someone stealing his credit," I said. "You said it yourself. This whole scheme to ruin Rosa's project. It's pretty impressive. He should already know that we think someone other than the king is behind the plot."

"That's why you were being so awkward downstairs," Ava said. "You knew he was listening through the robot."

Was awkward the word? I would've preferred clever. "Right. So, what if we start praising someone else for the whole operation? He won't be able to resist bragging."

My brother and sister were quiet. That was a good sign.

"I like it," Maya answered. "What do we need to do?"

"Are you guys in?" I asked my siblings.

Matt and Ava rolled forward in their chairs and extended their right hands. Matt laid his massive mitt on top of Ava's. I followed. Then we looked over at Maya. "Oh, we're really doing this?" she asked. "Okay then," she said, scooting in to complete the circle, "let's do it. I'm in."

19

OPERATION
TURKISH DELIGHT

BY LATE SUNDAY MORNING, THE SECOND DAY AFTER our return, everything was in place. And it had to be. The weather had finally cleared. *Ohana's* crew was sailing back to Kauai, and since Krumplitch had "borrowed" most of the fuel for his midnight escape and the underplane was still having engine troubles, Hank was arranging for another plane to come and get us. If we were going to get Steven to confess, we had to do it as soon as possible.

A group of us were sitting outside before lunch when Martha came racing up the trail, waving her arms and shouting. Her timing was perfect. Steven's morning lab hours had just begun. The prince was locked away in his room.

"Isn't she overacting a little?" Ava whispered to me.

"What's gotten into her?" Hank asked.

It felt weird leaving Hank out of our plot, but he said he didn't want to know. I shrugged.

"Is she having a fit of some kind?" Ashley wondered aloud. "What's she saying?"

"Something about birds, I think," Hank guessed.

Finally, Martha stopped a few paces away. Breathless, she pointed toward the eastern end of the island. "Back there . . . in the old settlement sites . . . birds."

"Birds? What sort of birds?" Hank asked.

"Don't say finches," Ashley muttered.

Martha pointed at the bazillionaire like they were playing a game of charades. "Yes! Nihoa finches . . . hatching."

"Are you serious?" Ashley asked. Martha nodded. "Okay. We better go have a look."

"A chance to see biodiversity in bloom? I'm there," Hank said.

Ava winked at me; she'd predicted Hank's excitement.

Ben was flashing his bright white smile. "You do realize, Ashley, that if new chicks hatch here, the conservation society will kick you off this island."

"We'll see," she said. "I don't want you islanders passing off some new flock of honeycreepers as a rare and precious species."

Rosa wasn't quite as eager, but Hank convinced her, and soon the two of them, along with Kildare, Ashley, Martha, and Ben, were paired up and speeding to the other side of Nihoa on Steven's ATVs, trailing clouds of gray and brown dust.

"She was convincing, right?" Maya said.

I turned to Ava. "Are we all set?"

My sister crouched and set her backpack on the ground in front of her, then pulled out her trusted drone, Fred. I hadn't seen Fred for a few days. Was it weird that I missed him? Never mind. Don't answer that.

Ava powered up the robot, then watched as it buzzed high above us. She swiped her finger along the cracked screen of her old smartphone.

"You're still using your old one?" Matt asked.

"Sentimental value," Ava replied.

Maya humphed. "She's sentimental?"

"About her robots," I said.

Without looking away from Fred, Ava added, "And a few people, too." She piloted the robot down the hill and landed it gently on a rock outcropping about a football field away. Then she showed Maya her screen, which had a live video of the surrounding territory. "Fred's our security camera. This way we'll know when they're coming back."

Matt was still staring at the dust clouds. "How long do we have? Once they see that the birds aren't actually hatching, they'll probably come back here, right?"

I hadn't thought of that. "Yes. We should hurry."

While I'd convinced everyone that my plan was inspired by *The Art of War*, this was only partially true. The whole deception thing? Totally. But my main strategy for forcing a confession actually came from the season finale of *Duck Detective*. In the show, the crafty fowl is trying to get a goat named James to admit that he'd been stealing jewelry from the farmer's wife. The duck had some evidence, but he didn't show it to the bearded criminal right away. Instead, he acted friendly with his suspect at first, building trust, then surprised him with the key item—a necklace he'd found in the goat's pen.

But we weren't ready for that step yet.

We hurried inside. Ava rushed upstairs, and the rest of us remained in the living room. We moved to the couches and waited. Maya sat across from Matt and me. The last I'd seen, Harriet was in the kitchen. According to Martha, though, all we needed to do was mention Steven's name a few times and the machine would move within range. "Steven," I said. "Steven."

We waited. Nothing happened.

"Steven," Matt called out, a little louder.

"Shhhhh," I said. "We don't actually want Steven himself to come. Not yet."

Maya jumped up off the couch, hurried over to the kitchen door, opened it slightly, and announced, "Steven is so amazing."

The whirr of Harriet's electric motors sent her scurrying back to her spot on the couch. The robot rolled into the room. With her hand down by her hips, out of Harriet's view, Maya gave me a thumbs-up. We were ready to go.

"What were you saying?" I asked Maya.

"That Steven is amazing."

"Totally," I said, "but I'm impressed with Martha."

"I know, right?" Matt added.

"How do you think she tricked the king into doing everything?"

Maya pushed her hair behind her ears and scooted forward to the edge of the couch. "Well, you can't just be intelligent, like Steven," she began. "You need a certain amount of . . . what's the word . . ."

"Cunning?" Matt asked.

"Exactly!" I said. "Steven is book smart. But he's not quite as cunning as I am. Or Martha, for that matter."

"He doesn't have that edge," Maya added.

"How did she know the king would fall for it?"

A door slammed upstairs. Hurried footsteps followed, and the prince raced down three steps at a time. He crossed the room with all the head-spinning fury of a miniature human tornado. Then he stopped, breathed, and clasped his hands behind his back. His small chest was puffed out. He smoothed out his hair.

"What's up?" Maya asked, casually.

Steven hesitated. "I was just—"

He couldn't admit that he was listening. So now he didn't know what to say. I raised my eyebrows and tried to look concerned. "Is something wrong, Steven?"

Ava's turn had come. And she delivered, right on time.

"Experiment number seventy-seven, ready," the robot announced.

To himself, Steven muttered, "Seventy-seven? What? That's not right." He reached around to the side of the robot.

Was he going to shut it off? That would not be good. I glared at Matt.

"What's wrong?" my brother asked him, stalling.

"There has been an upgrade," the robot said.

Steven stood up straight. "An upgrade?"

"A major upgrade," Harriet added. "What would you like to talk about?"

Steven stared at Matt. Then Maya. And, finally, me. Why was I last? He pointed to my brother. "Where's your sister? Has she been tinkering with my robot? If she added a single line of code . . ."

Matt held up his hands. "Hey, I don't know. Ava has a mind of her own."

"I didn't fix any bugs," Steven said to himself. "Who performed this upgrade? Which user?"

"A guest user," Harriet answered. "What would you like to talk about? The latest upgrade expanded my list of conversational topics."

Steven pushed back his sweat-matted hair. "But how did she . . ."

"We could discuss climate change, thermodynamics, the Higgs boson, the extinction of bison . . ."

Matt pressed his fist to his mouth, trying not to smile. Was it really funny? I don't know. Nerd jokes have their own rhythm.

Steven watched Matt, then answered, "A true intelligence test would not be confined to pre-chosen topics."

"Are you talking to us?" Maya asked.

"No," he snapped. "The machine."

The prince had his confidence back. He was standing taller. He stared at the ceiling. Then he turned to the robot and asked, "How about the sport of basketball?" he asked. "Let's talk about basketball."

This was bad. Ava knew nothing about basketball. That was my area. She could search for answers on the Internet, but she'd have to be quick.

"How about climate change instead?" Matt suggested.

"No," Steven answered. "Basketball is perfect." He lifted his chin. "Let's start with something simple. Who were the NBA champions in 2015?"

"I know that," I said. "The Golden State Warriors."

The robot repeated my answer.

"That hardly counted," Steven said. He paused. "And who is the league's best player?" he asked. "Quiet this time, Jack."

The question was not an exact one; it required an opinion. A judgment call. And machines don't have opinions. But Harriet was offering an answer before I had a chance to interrupt. The robot pronounced the name of the recent winner of the National Basketball Association's Most Valuable Player award. Steven spun around, walked straight up to his prized machine, and sneered in its mechanical face. "Did you look that up online, Ava?"

The prince was racing up the stairs before we could even react. I was frozen. My plan was ruined. "He wasn't supposed to figure it out that quickly," I muttered.

Maya and Matt jumped off the couches and chased after him. We caught up just as Steven was pushing through the door into his lab. Ava rolled away from the desk.

"Out of my chair," he demanded.

Ava looked at Matt and me. "Wrong answer?"

"A clear giveaway," Steven said. He dropped into his chair and spun to face us. "So, you figured out my little secret."

I glanced at the C-3PO poster behind him. No use

281

waiting any longer. "Not just your secret about Harriet," I said, then raced over, tore off the picture, turned back around, and smiled proudly at the overconfident brat. "What do you have to say about that?"

"Jack?"

"Admit it, Steven," I said. I laughed a little and held my shoulders back. This was my necklace-in-the-goat's-pen moment, and I was going to enjoy it. "It was you the whole time. You were the one who hired the submarine operator. You arranged for the king to flood the lab."

"You have no proof."

I pointed back over my shoulder. "Um, yes, I do."

"Jack?" Maya repeated. She pointed to the wall behind me. I turned. All the evidence was gone.

"You got rid of it?"

"I have no idea what you are talking about," he said with a smirk. Then he faced Ava and Matt. "That little trick you just pulled, impersonating my robot, trying to get me to think that you'd upgraded my machine. You tried to use Sun Tzu, didn't you? All warfare is based on deception? Well, if you had read closely, you would have taken note of verse twenty-six. Forgot that, did you? Why don't you tell the others what it says, Ava?"

I answered for her. "The general who makes the most calculations wins."

"Close, Jack," Steven said. "Very close." He closed his eyes as he recited the fragment. "'The general who loses a battle makes but few calculations beforehand. Thus do many calculations lead to victory, and few calculations to defeat.'" He opened his eyes. "That's the Giles translation, if you're wondering."

"What are you talking about?" Maya asked. "We all know it's you."

"I have been proven guilty of nothing," Steven replied. "Ashley will believe me, her only son, and none of you will have any way to prove otherwise, because I have made more calculations. You're not dealing with a simpleton here, people. You're dealing with a true genius."

Matt pointed to the computer screens. "We found the emails you sent to the king," he said.

The emails? What was he talking about?

"You found nothing."

"I traced them back to this machine," Ava said, "and I just forwarded the information to your mother."

She was lying. My siblings were both making this up. And it was working. Steven's eyes narrowed. His head tilted forward as if he was getting ready to charge us like a bull. He clenched and raised his fists. And then he let out a long and completely forced laugh. "You really think you outsmarted me? You're wrong! Wrong, wrong, wrong. What kind of fool would use his own computer? You, maybe," he said, pointing to me. "Or you," he said, pointing to Maya. "But certainly not me. You couldn't possibly have found those emails here. I logged into my mother's machine to send them, and I—"

Maya interrupted him, murmuring, "You, you just—"

"I just what?"

"You just confessed," Ava said.

"No, I didn't."

"You did," Matt added. "I heard it."

Ava turned her phone around to show him the screen. A timer was running. "I'm recording everything, Steven."

"I'll deny it!" Steven said. "All of it. Who do you think she'll believe? You people? Or her cherished only son? You have no proof, you ignorant fools!"

Maya pointed to Ava's phone. "I mean, we kind of do have proof now."

If a kid could have spontaneously exploded from anger, Steven would have done so right then and there. "I've had enough of all of you!" he shouted. "I want you all off our island immediately. Get on that ridiculous wooden raft again if you have to."

"Steven, it was you?"

His face turned white. Ashley was standing in the doorway. Her mouth formed a weak, disappointed smile. The energy that pulsed around the bazillionaire had faded. Hank stood behind her, and I heard Rosa and the others hurrying up the stairs. "What's happening here?" Hank asked. "Is everything okay?"

Maya pointed to Ava's cracked smartphone on the desk. She mouthed a question, "Fred?"

Our warning system had failed.

Ava winced. "Dead batteries," she replied.

"Ashley?" Hank asked.

The bazillionaire's only child fell back into the seat, staring up at his mother as she stood in the doorway. I wasn't sure if he was going to whimper or cry. But he was clearly beyond lying. That, at least, was finished, now that he'd been caught by the one person in his life whose opinion really, truly mattered to him.

"Why?" she asked. "Why would you sabotage such a beautiful prototype?"

Rosa stepped into view. "He did it? Your son?"

Steven ignored Rosa. "Why?! Are you seriously asking me why? I hate this place! Don't you know that? I've asked you to leave about a thousand times."

"You know I prefer such requests to come in writing, Steven," Ashley replied.

"I did write you! We've been stuck on this jagged tooth for eighteen months already!" He pointed to Maya. "If you

285

islanders hadn't been so incompetent, we would've been gone a year ago. But you just couldn't get the job done, so I had to find a way to make it work myself. I'm surrounded by adults and imbeciles." I squinted; he caught me. "See!" he said, pointing at me. "Imbeciles is another word for idiots, Jack."

"I know that, and I'm not an—"

Hank put his hand on my shoulder, then leaned down and whispered, "We know."

Steven leaned forward and clutched his head with both hands. He groaned with frustration toward the floor. "You don't understand me, Ashley. You never have. I'm not just some genius. Sure, I'm brilliant," he said, as if someone had corrected him. "But I want more. I want to do kid things. I want to go to real birthday parties, without piano recitals and coding sessions. I want to be on some kind of sports team. Or own one, at least." He glanced at me again, then Ava, Matt, and Maya. "I want . . . friends."

"But that's why they're here—"

"Not friends that you arrange. Real friends, Mom."

"You called me Mom."

"I'm sorry, I—"

She shivered. "No, no, I understand. Technically, I am your mother, but I really do prefer Ashley." Gazing down at her son, she breathed in through her nose, then lunged forward and extended her hand. Smiling, Steven clasped it in his own and they shook ferociously. Hank tried to push the two of them closer together, into an actual embrace, but mother and son both recoiled.

Ava looked up at Rosa. "Aren't you going to say something? He totally—"

The engineer held up her right hand and waved it toward them dismissively. "Not now," she said. "I'll let them have their moment."

"But he just admitted that he sabotaged the TOES," Matt noted. "We caught him."

"I know," Rosa said, "and I'm sure Ashley values this project and her son's reputation enough to ensure that both of them survive this terribly unfortunate mess." She winked at my siblings, who smiled with a mix of relief and delight.

Ashley let go of her son's hand. Both of them coughed and shook their heads and shoulders, ridding themselves of any remaining traces of emotion. She nodded to Rosa. "Understood," Ashley replied. Then she turned back to her son. "As for your distaste for this island, Steven, you'll be happy to hear that we are leaving anyway."

"What do you mean?" I asked. "Why?"

She flicked the fingers of her right hand toward the door. "Those stupid little birds are hatching," she said.

"Well, actually," I confessed, "we kind of made that up. We had to find a way to get you all out of here."

Now Martha appeared in the hall, breathless from running. "No, really, they're hatching," she said. "I saw them." She caught Steven glaring at her. "Well, what was I supposed to do?" she asked him.

"You told them?"

"No, they figured it out," she said. She pointed at me. "He did, actually."

Nothing could have disappointed Steven more. "You? You?"

"He's actually very intelligent," Hank said. "Just not in the normal, measurable sort of way."

Matt elbowed me. I felt my face turning red.

"Are you seriously blushing?" Steven asked.

"Rosa, honestly," Martha began, "I didn't know he was sabotaging the TOES. I figured his only scam was the mechanical—"

"Shhhh!" Ava said.

Martha looked back and forth between Steven, Matt, Ava, and me. "What?" she asked.

"We haven't really talked about everything," Matt said.

The tutor squinted, then nodded. My siblings were saving him from embarrassment. I don't know why. He definitely didn't deserve it. And it was kind of annoying that they were acting so . . . mature. But I wasn't going to stop them. "We've just been focused on the TOES," I added.

"So you didn't help him destroy the system?" Ashley asked the tutor.

"No! Honestly, that was all him."

Normally, I would've expected another flash of disappointment. Maybe a touch of anger. Instead, Ashley smiled with pride. She extended her hand and patted the air above Steven's head. "I'm impressed, young man. I wonder if we should consider a career in business instead of science."

Under her breath, Rosa moaned, "I'm having a really hard time not screaming right now."

"Fascinating," Hank said, studying the mother and son. "Truly fascinating."

Martha nodded to Maya. "Your grandfather saw the birds, too," she added.

"Which means," Ashley explained, "that the conservation society will be issuing an order for us to evacuate Nihoa immediately."

"Really?" Steven said.

"Really," she said. "You're getting your wish. What do you think, dear? Where should we live next? San Francisco? Los Angeles? Seattle?"

"Oh, I don't know," he said. I stared at my brother and

sister. Both were wide-eyed and terrified. A feeling of panic was rising within me as well. Even Hank looked frightened at what Steven might say next. In my head, I repeated the same phrase over and over, like a magician chanting a spell. Not New York. Not New York. Not New York. Steven cracked his knuckles and sighed with pleasure. "I was thinking of something on the East Coast, Ashley. What do you think of Brooklyn?"

All at once, Ava, Matt, Hank, and I shouted, "No!"

20

AN ABSOLUTE WRECK

WE DECIDED TO FLY OFF NIHOA THAT NIGHT, AND the seaplane Hank had sent for landed in the cove before dusk. Saying goodbye to the Hawkings was massively awkward. Do you thank someone who hosted you at their personal Hawaiian paradise if they almost got you killed? I don't know. None of us could really figure that one out. Down on the beach, Ashley offered us leis, the flowery wreaths that were meant to show affection and friendship. The tradition was to present them to guests upon arrival or departure. Hank was going to accept, but then he started sneezing, and the rest of us declined.

Maya and Rosa had come down to say goodbye, and Ben was on his way, too. The Hawkings retreated, allowing us to speak in semi-privacy. After Hank, Matt, and I all wished the engineer good luck, Ava held out her hand, and Rosa shook it affectionately. "Anytime you want to talk about school, engineering, life . . . anything . . . you let me know, okay?"

My sister wasn't ready to say goodbye to the engineer just yet. She didn't cry or anything, but she also wouldn't let go of Rosa's hand. Finally, Ava backed up and replied, "Right. Yes. I will."

I leaned toward Rosa and added, "We're not always so good with feelings."

A wave broke near the shore. We turned to watch the whitewater rushing over the sand. Matt was staring distantly at the ocean. "You seem . . . different," Hank said to him.

My brother smiled, then looked at Maya, Ava, and me before replying, "I wouldn't want to do it again, exactly. Getting lost out there. Or not quite like that. But I learned so much on the water."

Hank placed a hand on his shoulder. "You'll have to teach me sometime," he said.

The fireworks show at Steven's party hadn't gone as planned, but I could practically see colorful bursts of joy popping and streaking in the air around my brother's head. Hank wanted to learn from him? That was just about the greatest thing that could ever happen to Matt. But of course he tried to act like it was no big deal. He shrugged and said, "I'd like that."

"You can't leave yet!"

Ben was coming down the path, waving. I appreciated the interruption—this goodbye thing was getting a little too heavy.

"Why not?" Hank asked.

"Your teeth!" Ben said. "We'll give you a deal. Half off the regular price for a whitening."

Maya backhanded her grandfather on the shoulder. "Not now," she said.

"Maybe swimming tips, too?" Ben added.

They thought that was funny, but I was glad to see that Maya didn't laugh. She just smiled. Matt gave her the world's quickest hug, and then she looked at me, and I didn't know whether to try an even faster embrace, extend my hand, attempt a Hawking-style air-hug, or just turn and run and never look back. The last option was looking good when, in a tone just louder than a whisper, she asked, "Will you write to me, Jack?"

"Email, you mean? I can text, too. Or we could connect on social—"

She handed me a small, folded piece of paper. "Letters," she said. "I don't like screens. That's my address. You'll write me a letter?"

My mouth hung open but no words came out.

"He'll write you a letter," Matt said. "He's a great writer."

Next, Maya took one of the discarded leis from the grass,

293

walked over, and hung it around my neck. This time I accepted.

Almost nine months have passed since we left Nihoa. The birds did force Ashley off her island, and she really did fly her whole house away by helicopter, one container at a time. She and Steven moved to New York, too, but they settled into a huge townhouse in Manhattan, which might as well be another galaxy. I actually stay in touch with Steven. Sort of, anyway. We play Chicken Racer against each other online a few times a week. He's not bad. And yes, I do write to Maya, and three times she has even written back.

Matt is all into poetry again for some reason, and Ava messages with Rosa all the time. She says that Rosa is like a big sister, and she's always updating us on our engineer friend's progress. Apparently, Rosa talked Ashley into giving her twenty-five million dollars so she could get back to work on the TOES. She needed a few months to salvage some of the equipment before building a second prototype. This time, Ashley promised not to get involved, or let her son anywhere near the facility. In return, Rosa promised that no one would say anything at all about the sabotage. Everyone was quick to point out to me that this included anonymous tips to bloggers and members of the news media. As if I'd ever divulge the details of our adventures to anyone.

As for Albert Charles Krumplitch, he invested all of his savings into his idea for mobile, robotic air conditioners, and according to a story in the *Honolulu Times* that Maya packed in with one of her letters, the project was a total failure.

Me? All that talk about basketball inspired me to start practicing, but after a few days hanging around the courts near our apartment, jumping into games with the neighborhood kids, I found out they were only letting me play because they thought I was legally blind. I was too embarrassed to tell them I was just really uncoordinated, so I stopped going. After that, I signed up for a martial arts class. My kung fu career lasted a little longer, but not much. All I learned from the five classes I attended was that I don't like getting hit.

As for Hank, he was barely around at all that summer. He kept talking about the big new idea he'd thought up in Hawaii, but he still wouldn't give us any details, which was totally killing Matt. And I hadn't heard another word about exactly how I'd inspired him, either. We'd see him at the lab for a day, maybe two, but then he'd be gone for weeks. And he'd come back with a blistering tan.

One Monday morning before the start of the school year, Matt, Ava, and I walked over to Hank's lab together.

295

The heat of the day wasn't quite strangling yet, but I was sweating by the time we got to the secret entrance, which was hidden below a Dumpster in the alley across the street. Although we'd been working at Hank's lab for more than a year, this part never got old, and we took turns pressing the hidden button. My turn happened to be that day, and the blast of cool air that rushed up out of the underground tunnels nearly froze the beads of sweat on my forehead. As we rode down the escalators, I was thinking about jumping into the dive tank for a swim. Assuming Hank wasn't around.

Then we stepped through the doors into the lab.

The place was an absolute wreck.

Normally, the lab was impeccable. Keeping everything in order was one of my jobs. But now all the equipment had been flipped over or smashed. Robots were lying in crumpled, mangled heaps. The glass wall to the Mars simulation chamber was cracked. A puddle was stretching across the floor—the dive tank was leaking. Red lights were flashing. Electric motors were spinning aimlessly.

Ava rushed to a pile of metal and wires on the floor. It took me a minute to realize it was the smashed remains of one of Hank's flying robots. "Who could've done this?" she asked.

"And why?" Matt said, staring in awe at the damage.

Now, before I go on, let me be clear here. I wasn't happy about this little disaster. Not in the slightest. But I like to believe there's a bright side to almost everything. Sure, the lab was ruined. I'd probably have to spend two months cleaning.

But we did have a new mystery to solve.

ELEVEN ABSOLUTELY ESSENTIAL QUESTIONS ABOUT THE DEEP BLUE SEA

THE FAMOUS ASTRONOMER CARL SAGAN—BILL'S former professor—once called Earth the pale blue dot. From space, that's what our planet looks like. It's not the color of our fields and deserts and cities. No, Earth looks blue because the ocean covers roughly 71 percent of our planet's surface. (Check out the experiment for more.) And 90 percent of our biosphere, or the parts of Earth packed with life, is actually in the ocean. Yet we know so little about what goes on down there in the deep blue sea.

On the classic television show *Star Trek*, the captain of the starship refers to space as the final frontier. We're both major supporters of space exploration—Bill is the head honcho at the Planetary Society, an organization dedicated to the science and technology of studying other worlds. But there are also some amazing and unexplored territories right here on Earth. In many ways, our ocean might actually be the next great frontier for exploration. That's one of the reasons we decided to send Jack and crew on this latest adventure. We want to give you a chance to learn a little more about the deep blue sea, and we hope to inspire your interest in this fascinating subject. Plus we both really like Hawaii.

So here are a few questions and answers about Jack and the geniuses and their journey in and around that strange and fantastic world.

1. HOW MANY SPECIES LIVE IN THE WORLD'S OCEANS?

Scientists don't have an exact number. Some estimates suggest that we've found one million different species of plants and creatures in the ocean, and others say there might be another eight or nine million more we haven't discovered. But these aren't all fish like the sharks and bristlemouths we discuss in the book. If you scoop up a liter of seawater, for example, you might not see anything kicking or wriggling around. But more than 38,000 different microbes, too small for our eyes to see, will be hiding inside that sample of the ocean.

The deep ocean is full of life, too. According to a recent study called the Census of Marine Life, there are more than 17,000 different species living in the deep, out of sunlight's range.

2. HOW DEEP IS THE OCEAN? The deepest point is at the

bottom of the Mariana Trench in the Pacific Ocean—a

place known as Challenger Deep. It's more than 35,000 feet down, or as high as an airliner will fly above the ground. Mount Everest stands only about 29,000 feet tall.

3. HAVE SCIENTISTS EVER BEEN DOWN THERE? Yes! Repeatedly, in fact. The first real deep-sea adventurers were William Beebe and Otis Barton, who dropped down to 3,028 feet in 1934. (Hank mentions Beebe in the story.) But others have since made the even-more-daring trip down into the Mariana Trench. The movie director and explorer James Cameron piloted an amazing submarine called *Deepsea Challenger* to 35,787 feet below the surface, down to the bottom of the Trench.

4. IS *CHALLENGER* AS COOL AS *NAUTILUS REDUX*? Way

more amazing, actually. It's twenty-four feet tall and insulated with a foam material designed to resist the powerful water pressure at the bottom of the Trench. It has a so-called slurp gun that vacuums up interesting creatures for scientists to study at the surface. Plus it descends at a rate of 500 feet per minute. That's way faster than Jack and Ashley's trip.

5. WHY DON'T JACK AND ASHLEY HAVE TO TAKE THEIR TIME TO GET TO THE SURFACE, LIKE SCUBA DIVERS? Divers need to rise slowly because they're breathing compressed air that has been squeezed and jammed into their SCUBA tanks. Some of the nitrogen in the air leaks out of their lungs into other parts of their body. If they rise to the surface too quickly, then some of those compressed air bubbles expand as the water pressure around them drops, which can be extremely painful and harmful. But submarines have systems that generate, recycle, and filter air so their crews don't have to breathe the same stuff you'd get from a SCUBA tank. Remember how Jack complains about the air inside the *Nautilus Redux* being dry? That's because of this filtration and recycling system.

6. IS MARINE POOP REAL? Yes. Honestly. That's not just aquatic bathroom humor.

7. WHICH GADGETS AND INVENTIONS MENTIONED IN THE STORY ARE REALISTIC? We don't know of anyone who has made shoelaces out of spider silk. But scientists have been working for years to find ways to artificially produce this amazing material, which can be stronger than steel. This approach to invention is called biomimicry. Basically, it involves borrowing nature's best tricks. The slippery coating that causes Jack to fall off the side of Hank's building in *At the Bottom of the World* is one such example. Artificial spider silk is another.

The weight-loss high-tops that Jack wears are definitely possible, too, but a step-counting pedometer like the Fitbit is far more practical. And while the idea of someone building their own deep-sea submersible might seem unbelievable, Hank's *Nautilus Redux* is based on a real story. An inventor and captain named Karl Stanley designed his own submarine, *Idabel*, which can dive to more than two thousand feet.

Okay, but what about a kid building his own nuclear reactor? Strangely enough, that's real, too. Greg once interviewed a teenager who spent two years designing a homemade reactor, and he wasn't the first or last kid to accomplish this dangerous feat. But we don't suggest trying it yourself. Really.

8. IS THE TOES A REAL SYSTEM? Technically, this method of generating electricity is known as Ocean Thermal Energy Conversion, or OTEC. Engineers have successfully tested small prototypes that work in much the same way as our fictional TOES does in the story, but no one has yet built one out at sea. Maybe they need a bazillionaire's help.

302

9. CAN YOU ACTUALLY USE THE STARS TO NAVIGATE, THE WAY MAYA AND MATT DO? The practice of what's known as celestial navigation, or determining your position based on the paths of the stars through the sky, has been used for thousands of years. All that stuff Maya says about how her ancestors used the stars to sail the oceans is completely true. Historians believe that this is how the ancient Polynesian people discovered the Hawaiian islands in the first place. They didn't have GPS. Their maps were in the stars, and just like Maya, they were able to interpret the ocean currents, the directions of the waves, and the way the light changed on the horizon to find their way to distant islands.

10. IS NIHOA ISLAND A REAL PLACE? Yes, but we changed a few details. And we're pretty sure no billionaires live there. Nihoa is one of the Leeward Islands north of Hawaii. Our interest in Nihoa stems from Bill's own knowledge of Wake Island, another in the Leeward chain. His father was stationed on Wake Island during World War II, and he was a member of a group of civilians who defended the territory from Japanese attacks.

II. DO PEOPLE REALLY DRINK CAULIFLOWER JUICE? Greg tried some, as research for the book, and he doesn't recommend it, but you could always write to him for the recipe.

OUR BIG
BLUE OCEAN

BY BILL NYE

SURE, I COULD TELL YOU HOW MUCH OF THE EARTH'S surface is covered with water. Or you could hitch a ride to the International Space Station, stare back at our planet, and get a sense for yourself. But how about a simple home experiment instead?

MATERIALS

A basketball

A roll of 2.5-cm-wide (that's an inch, for those of you who haven't been converted to the metric system yet) masking tape or blue painter's tape

A friend, or friendly sibling

STEPS

1. Grab the basketball and the roll of tape. The blue painter's tape is ideal, since it will remind you of the ocean.

2. Start unrolling the tape and keep doing it until you

measure out 517 centimeters. That's 203 inches. To prevent it from getting tangled, do this in pieces, and stick the fragments to the edge of a counter or table. Just make sure you keep track.

3. Now have some fun. Break up the tape into smaller pieces and stick them anywhere you can on the ball. The only rule is that no two pieces of tape can overlap.

4. When you're finished, turn the ball around in your hands. The tape represents water, while the leathery spots represent the dry areas of our planet's surface. The ratio of tape to leather is the same as the ratio of water to dry land on Earth.

5. Try playing catch with your friend without touching the tape. Make sure he or she isn't on their phone first, though. You wouldn't want to hit them in the face with a planet.

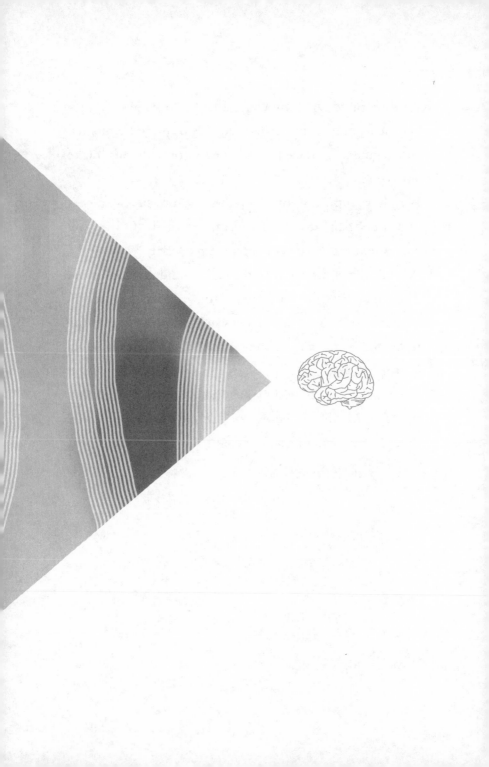

ABOUT THE AUTHORS

BILL NYE IS **A SCIENCE EDUCATOR**, mechanical engineer, television host, and *New York Times* bestselling author with a mission: to help foster a scientifically literate society and help people everywhere understand and appreciate the science that makes our world work. Nye is best known for his Emmy award–winning children's television show, *Bill Nye the Science Guy*, and for his new Netflix series, *Bill Nye Saves the World*. As a trusted science educator, Nye has appeared on numerous television programs, including *Good Morning America*, *CNN New Day*, *Late Night with Seth Meyers*, *Last Week Tonight with John Oliver*, and *Real Time with Bill Maher*. He currently splits his time between New York City and Los Angeles. Follow him online at www.billnye.com.

GREGORY MONE IS A NOVELIST, science journalist, and speaker who has written several books for children, including *Fish* and *Dangerous Waters: An Adventure on the Titanic*, and a few books for adults, too. He lives on Martha's Vineyard, Massachusetts, with his family. Follow him online at www.gregorymone.com.

IN CASE YOU
MISSED IT